"B-but your—hair! It's gone—green!" (*page 62*).

# JILL MAKES GOOD

*by*
ELIZABETH TUGWELL

*Illustrated by*
SALLY CRAVEN

THOMAS NELSON AND SONS, Ltd.
*London, Edinburgh, Paris, Melbourne*
*Toronto, and New York*

THOMAS NELSON AND SONS LTD
Parkside Works Edinburgh 9
3 Henrietta Street London WC2
312 Flinders Street Melbourne C1
5 Parker's Buildings  Burg Street  Cape Town

THOMAS NELSON AND SONS (CANADA) LTD
91–93 Wellington Street West   Toronto 1

THOMAS NELSON AND SONS
385 Madison Avenue New York 17

SOCIÉTÉ FRANÇAISE D'EDITIONS NELSON
25 rue Henri Barbusse Paris Vᵉ

# CONTENTS

# CONTENTS

# CHAPTER I

### HOW IT ALL BEGAN

GILLIAN ROSS grinned her mischievous curly grin as she poked her head out of the taxi window and said hopefully, "Oh, Lambie darling, won't it be gorgeous if I miss my train! And I believe I'm going to." Her sparkling blue eyes looked very gleeful as she gazed round her at the traffic block in which the taxi seemed wedged as if it were never going to move again.

If Jill lost the Cornish Express at Paddington

that would put off her going to Aunt Pamela for a few days at least, she thought to herself; but, of course, Lambie, her old Nannie, would not see any delay, however small, as the respite it was.

But kind old Lambie—Mrs. Lambert was her real name—understood much better than Jill thought she did, for she gave the girl's hand an encouraging squeeze, and said : " Look on the bright side, ducky, and remember this : if you write me a line I'll come, whether it's from Cornwall or the other side of the world."

This was comforting news, and Jill felt as if the sun had come out, for Lambie was the one bit of home the fourteen-year-old girl had left. She sat back in her seat and pulled her black beret further on to her tousled curly bob of bright red hair, and decided that perhaps things were not so bad after all.

Click, click went the taxi meter totting up the pennies, and then the lorry in front of them moved on, and their taxi could jerk forward again.

When they got to Paddington they were terribly late, and the engine was puffing as if it were a live thing and impatient to be off. Jill rushed to the ticket office ; Lambie caught a porter and had the luggage labelled at top speed, and then they sprinted down the long

*They sprinted down the long platform.*

platform as if they were training for the hundred
yards.

How they did it they never knew, for the train

was already beginning to move, but luckily one of the carriage doors was still swinging open. Before the guard could bang it Jill shot inside with a wild leap, and the porter hurled her cases in after her.

The girl picked herself up, for her frantic rush had landed her almost on to the lap of a stout lady with a fat Pekingese. Turning in a flash, Jill slammed the window down and poked her head out. " Bye-bye, Lambie ! " she cried as sportingly as she could, in spite of the tears that would blur her eyes as she saw the short sturdy figure of her old Nannie, with her old-fashioned hat, grow smaller and smaller on the dwindling platform.

" If you don't mind closing that window," said a voice behind her, " and moving your suit-case from my feet."

It was the lady with the Pekingese, and she really had a grievance. Jill's cheeks flamed, for it was horrible being caught by a stranger looking blue. She grabbed her case hurriedly and thrust it under the seat. Then, though it seemed a shame on such a lovely March morning, she pulled up the window obediently, and settled down for a long spell of gazing out. She had seldom been out of London, and the long journey down to Cornwall had all the spice of novelty.

Soon the train ran out of the grimy city into

pale spring sunshine, and the neat suburban roads gave place to fields with little wobbly new baby lambs in them.

Lunch was very pleasant, and the book of school stories Lambie had bought her whiled away the afternoon, but when Jill had demolished the contents of her tea basket, time began to hang heavy.

She had the carriage to herself now, for the lady with the Pekingese had got out at Plymouth, and Jill pressed her tired face against the glass and wondered how much she liked this sweep of fields, and moor, and hills dotted with the white mounds of the china-clay works that flashed past.

" Ugh ! why does Aunt Pamela live here ? " she thought.

Leaning forward, with her chin cupped in her hands, Jill set herself to remember all she could about this young auntie with whom she was going to live now that she had no Mummy and no home of her own any more.

Auntie Pamela was very clever, the girl knew, for she wrote crook yarns and thrillers of all kinds, and Jill had sometimes seen her name, Pamela Merrick, on the covers of magazines.

About a year ago she had migrated to a cottage in Cornwall and acquired a secretary-companion, Miss Trevone, who was reported to have travelled such a lot, and spoke so many

languages that Jill felt sure she must be about
ninety in order to have had time for so many
varied experiences.

For one reason or another Jill had seen so
little of her aunt, darling Mummy's young
sister, that she was an almost unknown quantity
to the girl, and in her heart of hearts poor Jill
felt rather like the people in the pirate stories
when they know they are soon to step off the
end of the plank.

"Well, I'll know the worst in a minute now,"
she said to herself as she jumped up, for the train
was slowing down.  "Auntie said Miss Trevone
would meet me at Saint Pennah's Halt with the
car."

And then the train drew up at the smallest,
funniest station in the world.

Jill grabbed her suit-case and jumped out.
She looked expectantly up and down the platform, but it was deserted except for two country-
women with bags and bundles, and a man who
leaned against the ticket office and smoked.

"How queer!" exclaimed Jill.  "Miss Trevone hasn't come to meet me.  What shall I
do?"

Suddenly a young girl with a bright red beret
pulled down over tumbled brown curls and a
small piquant face, dashed up.  "Tell me," she
said pleasantly, "are you Gillian Ross?"

" Yes, I'm Jill ; and you—you're——? "

" I'm Vivien," she cried as she kissed her impulsively ; " and I'm awfully glad you've come. Now where is the baggage ? What have you got ? "

" A trunk and a bag, besides these."

" Oh, help ! " Vivien whistled in dismay. " Eric will strike."

" Who is he ? " thought Jill. " The chauffeur, I expect."

Vivien wrinkled up her forehead as she stared mournfully at the big black trunk standing up on end in front of her, then a look of relief overspread her thin face. " I have it ! " she cried as she ran away. " Jim ! Hi, Jim ! " she called.

A second later she came back with a tall sandy-haired lad of about sixteen. " Jim, I'm in a fix," she began, " for this trunk simply must come on, and you know what Eric is. Could you take it for me, I wonder, in your cart ? "

" Surely, missie," he grinned, touching his cap. " I'll be along some time for sure, barring accidents."

" Some time ! " thought Jill, who felt as if she had got to the world's end. " And my pyjamas are in it."

Vivien thanked the boy, and then, fumbling in the pocket of her well-worn tweed coat, she

fished out a paper bag and handed it round.
" I say, I forgot these ! " she exclaimed. " Do
you like bulls' eyes, Jill ? They are awfully
comforting when it's cold," she added.

As Jill took a sweet their eyes met. " Well,
whoever Vivien is, she seems a sport," thought
Jill. " I shan't mind a bit about that frumpy
old Miss Trevone if only Vivien lives near enough
for us to have fun together sometimes."

Vivien was very small and slight ; her scarlet
beret only just reached the tip of Jill's ear ; and
yet Jill was sure she was nearly grown up, though
she would have been hard put to it to say why.
Perhaps it was the look in Vivien's big greeny-
grey eyes, with their dark lashes, or it might have
been her direct, assured way of speaking. " As
if she would fall on her feet if you dumped her
down in Patagonia," thought Jill suddenly, as
she picked up her case and followed the other
girl out of the station to a cobbled yard at the
back, where an old battered baby car with a
torn canvas hood was waiting.

" Allow me to introduce Eric, or Little by
Little," Vivien chuckled, drawing off the rug
in which its snout was muffled. " Hop in, please.
Sorry, you'll have to squeeze up a bit, or the
packages won't go in."

" And that old thing is Aunt Pamela's car ? "
thought Jill as she wedged herself in obediently.

Vivien bent to the cranking-handle in front. " The self-starter has gone west," she announced. " It is another case of C.A."

" What's C.A. ? "

" Can't afford ! " blurted out Vivien. Then she flushed and checked herself. " Oh bother, my hateful tongue again. Still, you'll have to know some time. But it's a shame, when Pam is such a sport."

Jill opened her eyes. " Do you call her Pam ? " she cried.

" Yes, and she doesn't mind. I simply couldn't say Miss Merrick now."

At this moment Eric gave a quiver, and woke into rattling life. Vivien jumped in, turned round, and waved good-night to Jim, who was laboriously hoisting the trunk on to his open farm cart. Then the overloaded little car was flying down a narrow stony road that wound between tall leafless hedges. A high March wind was grinding and tearing the twigs to pieces, and where the hedge was lower, or there was a gate, eddying gusts caught at the old blue car. It would have swerved but for Vivien's small strong hands on the wheel. Over and above the rushing of the wind Jill heard the roar of an angry sea breaking on rocks and hard sands.

" I wonder if I shall like Cornwall," she said doubtfully.

Vivien grinned. " You won't be able to help it," she answered.

" Have you lived here always ? " asked Jill.

Vivien shook her head. " No, not always," she answered in a final sort of way that put an end, somehow, to Jill's questions, and a silence fell.

" Though Vivien is not nearly as tall as I am," thought Jill, " when she looks at me with those great greeny-grey eyes of hers, she makes me feel almost afraid of her. Who on earth can she be ? "

" I suppose Miss Trevone wasn't very well " —Jill's curiosity got the better of her shyness at last—" so she asked you to come instead. Do you live near ? "

Vivien almost let go of the steering-wheel in astonishment. " But I am Miss Trevone ! " she exclaimed as she exploded with laughter. " I thought you knew."

" Aren't you—" stammered Jill, too astonished to be tactful, " rather young to be a——"

" A secretary-companion," answered Vivien. " I am. But things happened like that."

" I'm awfully glad you are you," Jill blurted out thankfully. " I was dead sure Miss Trevone would be elderly, and grumpy, and horrid."

The roar of the sea was louder now, and the bare upland fields had given place to open moorland. Vivien pointed away to the right. " Nothing will grow on the crest there," she said.

" Only withered grass and heather, with grey boulders cropping out like almonds on a cake. And there is a cairn, Jill ! It's rather *queer*. They say," she added, dropping her voice, " that the Piskies dance there, and that it is because it has belonged to them always that nothing people plant will thrive."

Jill shuddered deliciously. " Piskies ? Do you mean fairies ? "

Vivien nodded. " That cairn is a funny place, anyhow. No one knows who built it."

" I believe *you* half believe in them," said Jill ; but Vivien did not answer, and drove on fast. Presently, at the top of a hill so steep that it seemed to Jill to go straight down like the precipices in her geography books, Vivien jammed on her brake.

In front was the sweep of a rocky bay, into which a cruel grey sea was dashing its white breakers. Far out on the horizon one little sail was caught by the last red of the setting sun that dipped down into a ragged mass of dark cloud. The outlines of the distant headland were blurred in the lessening light, and the masses of gorse beside the road were dusky formless shapes. Close at hand, with a harsh cry and a flash of white wings, a belated gull swooped down.

Vivien, leaning forward, pointed eagerly.

Jill, peeping over her shoulder, saw, almost on

the edge of the sands, a little dark patch that was a house ; a light shone in the window as if to welcome them.

" That's home," said Vivien.

And from something in her tone Jill knew it was going to be her home too.

# CHAPTER II

VIVIEN released her brake and they slithered slowly down the steep lane. "Are we going to turn upside down ? " Jill wondered, feeling the little car slant to the left as they crept round the bend by the dead sloe tree. But to her great surprise they got to the bottom all right, and then Jill found that the road wound across a stretch of marshy land, where a shallow river raced over the stones, and then spread itself out across the sands.

Away to right and left stretched black cliffs with reefs and fallen boulders at their feet ; the incoming waves swept far across the sands in long tongues of foam, and the rising wind whistled creepily in the long grass of the dunes.

" Why, the house is almost on the beach ! " cried Jill.

" Yes, when we get a wind dead on to the land it sounds as if the waves were coming into the garden," answered Vivien. " Pam and I have sat sometimes, watching great clots of foam fly past the window—just listening, and scared stiff of what we might hear."

" How beastly ! " exclaimed Jill. " What were you expecting ? "

" Distress signals out at sea."

Jill did not see the house, with its squat chimney stacks, square windows, and jutting box-like porch, until she was almost there ; once they left the marsh behind them the hedges shut them in.

" Toot, toot, tootle ! My signature tune," laughed Vivien as she braked sharply.

On the instant, as if some one on the other side had been listening eagerly, the door opened, and Jill saw her aunt's tall slim figure framed in the lighted doorway. Then a fat black spaniel, barking loudly, cannoned down the garden path and frisked up to Jill, wagging his stumpy tail very fast indeed.

" Squibb is a friendly old thing, in spite of all the noise he makes when he hears the car ! " cried Miss Merrick. She ran down the garden path and put her arms round Jill, not a bit as if it were polite to kiss her because she was a relation, but as if she loved and wanted her very much.

Jill's heart went out to her. " Oh, Auntie dear," she said, returning the hug, " I'm glad I've come ! "

" Darling, I'm glad too."

Vivien, watching them from the gate, turned quickly and rooted violently among the packages on the back seat of the car. " And I'm nobody's niece," she thought. " Everything will be different now." For Vivien owed very much to Miss Merrick, who had taken her away from loneliness and given her a home. She had been at her wit's end, and then, marvellously, Pam had come on the scene. But Vivien was a sport, and she trampled on her jealousy quickly as she said to herself, " Poor old Jill has had a rotten time, and she must be fagged out. I'll jolly well be decent to her."

" Pam, darling ! " she called cheerfully. " You're not to keep Jill shivering out there. Take her in at once."

" Vivien is right," laughed Aunt Pamela. " The wind is bitter. Come in, and take your things off. Supper is ready, and I'm sure you must be famished." Hooking her arm through Jill's she drew the girl indoors.

A trifle shyly Jill followed her into a lamp-lit hall, with a grey flagged floor, and whitewashed walls on which two modern-looking water-colours hung, that caught her eyes at once.

" Those are Vivien's pictures," explained Miss Merrick.

" Auntie ! " Jill went across and looked at

them, amazed. " You don't mean Vivien paints
as well as that ? " she cried.

Miss Merrick nodded. " Yes, they are extra-
ordinarily good," she said warmly. " Vivien is
like her father."

" What did he do ? " asked Jill.

" He was an artist, and very nearly a genius.
Oh, it seems a waste," Miss Merrick went on,
half to herself. " There she is banging out my
tales of crooks and gunmen on her typewriter,
when she ought to be in a studio."

Miss Merrick was tall and very slim, with a
pretty fair face and a pair of wide grey eyes
fringed with long lashes ; her mouth was sweet,
and her brown hair waved back from her face
and was rolled into a knot at the nape of her
neck. Altogether she was a most satisfactory-
looking young auntie, and quite up to expecta-
tions, thought Jill.

When the girl had taken off her coat and
scrubbed the grime of the journey off her hands,
Aunt Pamela took her into the sitting-room, now
the dining-room as well, since Miss Merrick,
when she took the house, had turned the little
parlour into a study. Jill could not see much,
for the daylight was nearly gone, but a big wood
fire burned with a queer bluish flame on the hearth,
and when her aunt had lit the old-fashioned brass
lamp Jill saw a real country supper table.

Set out on the clean white cloth was a dish of pilchards and a crisp brown pasty that smelled most invitingly; a huge saffron cake and a crusty loaf of home-made bread were simply asking to be eaten, with generous dollops of Cornish cream. And when she saw all these good things Jill realized that her picnic tea had been finished hours ago, and that the long drive in the keen salt air had made her hungrier than she had ever been at home.

There had been just Mummy, Jill, and Lambie in the tall London house, for Jill could not remember her doctor father who had died when she was a baby. Lambie had been her Nannie then, and she had stayed with gentle little Mrs. Ross ever since.

Everything had seemed as if it were going on for ever, and fourteen-year-old Jill had fretted against the dullness of her little day-school, often saying almost resentfully that nothing thrilling ever seemed to happen.

And so her headmistress let her try for one of the scholarships to Beechdene Hall, that famous school founded more than a hundred years ago in a Dorset manor house, and kept vigorously up to date.

Jill had been thrilled by the idea; they had entered her name on the waiting-list, and in due time she had sat among a crowd of strange girls in a vast echoing classroom, and wrestled for three weary hours with an entrance examination paper that seemed to her quite impossibly hard.

On the day Jill heard she had failed, her mother took her to the pictures to cheer her up. Afterwards, coming out of the hot stuffy cinema into fog and sleety rain, Mummy, who was never very strong, caught a bad cold.

The next few days were dreadful ; the doctor came at night as well as in the morning, and Lambie never seemed to go to bed. Then in the dawn, so suddenly that there was no time even to wire for Auntie Pamela, the end came, and tired little Mrs. Ross laid her head on Lambie's shoulder and died like a child that had gone to sleep.

Before poor frightened Jill could realize anything, the old family lawyer, who was also her guardian, was on the scene ; he said that Lambie must get another place, for the house would have to be sold. Jill was to go and live with her Aunt Pamela in far-away Cornwall, and stay there all term-time, as well as the holidays, because there was not enough money for her to go to boarding-school if she wanted to have any left when she was twenty-one.

Jill privately could not imagine herself ever being such a vast age as twenty-one, and she would have plumped for school, if she had been asked, which of course she was not.

Coming here had been a rather horrid plunge, like diving into the deep end of the swimming-bath for the first time, but as she looked round her at the pretty, shabby room in the lamp-light, Jill thought that things were turning out not so badly after all.

# CHAPTER III

## SETTLING DOWN

NEXT morning the rushing of the sea and the beating of rain-drops on her window came to Jill through a tangle of vivid, broken dreams. For a second she lay with closed eyes, unable to recollect where she was, then remembrance came to her with a rush, and she jumped out of bed and ran to the window.

" Oh, what a hateful place ! " she said as she drew the curtains aside and peeped out.

A blanket of fog filled the tiny bay, blurred the softly breaking waves, and blotted out the headland. Somewhere a cow lowed dismally.

Pushing up the sash, Jill poked her head out and looked down at the little garden ; the tamarisk hedge glistened with rain ; the square of grass was sodden, but in the sheltered bed beside the house dozens of pale-green points, that were going to be lovely things soon, showed their tips above the black soil. But Jill was too much of a town girl to understand, and when a rain-drop went plop on her head, she drew back quickly, and stared about her with distaste at the small white and green room. " Ugh ! Only painted furniture and no carpet," she yawned. " I wish I had worked harder and won that scholarship. Auntie Pam is sweet, of course, and Vivien seems a real sport, though queer, but it will be as dull as tombs if I've got to be stuck here all the time with no hockey or anything."

Suddenly an odd ghostly sort of whisper behind her made her jump. " Hurry up ! " it said, " or I'll come in and throw something at you."

" Scoot ! " Jill answered, feeling cheered up all of a sudden. " I've got a wet sponge here."

Vivien abandoned the keyhole and scuttled away in mock terror as the breakfast bell rang.

Jill got dressed at lightning speed, and as she ran downstairs she found that a simply thrilling smell of fried bacon was in the air. Squibb, the fat black spaniel she had made friends with last night, came waggling up to greet her ; but she had no eyes for him at the moment, for there, looking so big and square that it seemed to fill the hall, was her trunk. " Oh, hooray ! " she cried.

" I knew Jim would not let us down," cried Vivien, turning from the hall door with letters in her hands. " He brought it last night after you were asleep. Now come along in to break- fast," she added, opening the door.

A shabby, welcoming room it was, with a miscellaneous collection of solid, comfortable chairs ; and a low chintz-covered seat that ran the whole way along below the wide bow-window looking out to sea. "Just the place to curl up and write to Lambie," thought Jill, and then she was kissing Aunt Pamela and being asked how she had slept.

Grace was said, and they all took their places at the round table laid with big satisfying-looking blue cups, a crusty brown loaf, a big dish of eggs and bacon, faintly sizzling still, and a pat of yellow butter with a cow stamped on it.

That almost black, highly polished table was one of Miss Merrick's treasures, and she had bidden for it at the sale of things from an old farmhouse. It fairly screamed at the cheap modern sideboard that offended Vivien every time she saw it, wishing that Can't Afford had not such a stranglehold on things.

Jill, feeding the eager slobbering Squibb with large bits of everything when no one was looking, decided that breakfast was a jolly sort of meal. The eats were topping, of course, and her aunt, in a soft hand-knitted jumper and well-worn grey tweed skirt, seemed hardly any older than Vivien.

Miss Merrick helped them to large platefuls

of everything, and filled their second cups of coffee for them, then, perching her horn-rimmed spectacles on her nose, she picked up her letters. " Excuse me, girls," she murmured, waving a vague hand over the good things on the table, " and help yourselves."

Vivien, with her little face alight with interest, squirmed forward in her chair as Pam passed the first envelope across for her to see.

To Jill, the literary talk that followed seemed to be that of another world where editors walked as human beings.

At last Miss Merrick got up, and going into the study she shut the door firmly. Vivien, bringing her mind back to the present with a jerk, remarked, " That means that genius burns ! Oh, if only Pam could chuck those yarns of derring-do and get down to her book."

" You don't mean Auntie is writing a book ! " gasped Jill.

" Yes. I've typed part of it, and it's great ! But our crooks and gunmen keep us in bread and butter, and Eric in petrol, so she has to stick to them. It's a fearful tax sometimes, and it is rotten luck, for it means that Pam comes to the book her heart is in, too tired to do it justice. Now then, Jill," Vivien jumped up with a change of tone, " let's fire away with your unpacking."

The trunk, even with the help of Cook, stubbornly refused to go upstairs, so Vivien half unpacked it and littered the hall with its contents, while Jill and Cook hauled it up half empty after fearful struggles.

Vivien, grabbing an armful of garments ran on ahead, and tossed them, half absently, into the dressing-table drawer. "Now we'll soon be done," she cried.

"Vivien!" expostulated Jill, who was fresh from Lambie's tidy ways.

"Sorry.  Never could be tidy," Vivien laughed reminiscently.  "I'm afraid a fearful lot of method has rolled off me like water off a duck's back!  You see, Daddy and I never bothered, and we were very happy.  If we did lose anything we always found it when we packed up to go, so it didn't seem to matter.  Whenever I look back we always seem to have been sitting on a trunk to make it shut, or else arriving somewhere."

"Where did you go to?"

"Oh, France and Italy and Spain; once we went to Germany, and we had six months in Roumania."

"Who do you mean by 'we'?" asked Jill.

"Just Daddy and I.  We had such fun," Vivien added softly.  "Oh, Daddy!  He would make anything seem to be fun, even arriving tired in a leaky bus on a rainy night."  She

turned and went out of the room to fetch some
more clothes, leaving Jill with her curiosity
thoroughly roused.

" How awfully queer," she thought. " Vivien
is younger than several of the big girls at school,
and she talks about places I've only met in
geography books as if they were just round the
corner ! And now she is in a real job, earning
her living. It's the weirdest thing I've ever
struck, and I'll jolly well get to the bottom of
it, if I can."

At that moment Vivien came flying back with
a sponge bag and some jumpers. " I say, be a
sport and tell me——" Jill began.

" Tell you—what ? " Vivien faced her blankly.

" What you did after you left Roumania, or
wherever it was. And how you came to live with
Auntie."

Vivien bit her lip, but she answered gently
enough.

" I will, one day, when we know each other
better."

Jill's tongue ran away with her. " I think you
are too jolly mean for words. You tell me half
the story, and then shut up as tight as wax.
Your Pam, as you call her, is my aunt, and you
are her secretary, so you ought to do what I
say."

Vivien, in whose mind jealousy was working

like a ferment, turned crimson to the tips of her ears. She dropped the handkerchief satchet she had tucked under her arm straight on to the heap of woollies at her feet, snatched up a nightdress of her own which she had lent Jill the night before, and tore out of the room, banging the door.

"Whew!" said Jill to herself as she shook out her frocks, and began to put them in the wardrobe. "Now I don't suppose Vivien will touch me with the tongs again. And she was jolly decent in lending me things last night when my trunk hadn't come. I've been rather a poisonous little pig, really. I wonder if she will be friends again? I don't know; anyhow I'll try."

And impulsively, as she did everything, Jill ran and tapped on Vivien's door. She did not turn her head as Jill entered, but something in her attitude as she stared out at the breaking clouds suggested hurt feelings rather than resentment.

Jill's quick eyes took in the room without realizing that she did. It said "home," but it did not suggest England. A length of vivid peasant embroidery covered the bed; seven portly little carved bears processed along the mantelpiece. On the opposite wall there hung cheaply framed water-colours; one was unfinished, but two were so lovely that Jill caught her breath. The shade was so shady; the plastered houses so dazzlingly white; they could have been painted nowhere else but in Spain.

The tumbled heap of clothes lying on the chair, just as Vivien had thrown them down, hurt Jill somehow.

" I can be an odious pig sometimes ! " Jill stammered out. " And I went one better than my best just now ! Will you forget, and be friends again ? "

Vivien fought a little fight with herself, then she held out her hand. " Yes," she said a trifle unsteadily.

Jill blinked quickly. " I didn't mean it— really," she said. " Don't tell Auntie."

" I won't," Vivien flashed back. " You went to a rather potty little day-school, I suppose, or you wouldn't talk like that."

It was Jill's turn to flush.

" Yes," she admitted frankly; " the one I was at was pretty mouldy. And then, when they let me try for the Beechdene scholarship, I just ragged, and played the goat, and of course I didn't pass."

" Hard luck." Vivien's heart warmed to Jill for this open admission. " But don't you get a second chance at the entrance exam. ? "

Jill nodded. " Yes, one other chance. But it is so fearfully stiff. Honestly, Vivien, I couldn't begin to guess at the answers to half the questions."

Vivien flopped down on the side of her bed. "H'm," she said, "I see. And I'd help you work for it like a shot, only the worst of it is my own education is a thing of shreds and patches. Mother died when I was eight, and Daddy and I moved about too much for me to go to school, or even have settled lessons for very long. He said I had read everything I could lay hands on since I was five, and could chatter in about four languages, so what did spelling matter? But I pretty soon found it did," she added sadly, "as soon as I found myself on my own. However, that's that." She added after a little pause, "Is the scholarship you did not win the only one for Beechdene?"

Jill shook her head. "No," she said, "there's another, called the Faith Anderson."

"Would it be any good to you?" asked Vivien.

"Not a hope!" replied Jill. "That other scholarship is a queer sort of thing. My head-mistress told me about it, though of course it is quite out of my line. You see, ages ago there was a girl at Beechdene called Faith Anderson, and she plunged into a canal and fished out a poor little crippled kiddie. It was in the winter, with lots of ice about. Faith was home for the

Christmas holidays, I think, and she was dreadfully ill afterwards, for weeks and weeks. Her people were fearfully rich, and so jolly thankful when she got well again that they gave a scholarship to the school and called it after her. It is to be given to ' Any girl who saves a life at the risk of her own—or acts with conspicuous bravery in circumstances of extreme difficulty or danger.' I've remembered the words exactly, because I always felt it would be—such a splendid sort of thing to win," Jill said awkwardly. " It is open every term, but I don't believe any one has won it for ages. Chances like that simply don't come to people," added Jill regretfully.

But Vivien was white to the lips. She clenched her hands in her lap to keep them from shaking, and said in a strange little broken voice, " Sometimes they do—and the people who do the rescuing don't always get well."

" Girls, it's nearly lunch time," called Miss Merrick from the foot of the stairs, and as Jill ran across the landing and leaned over the banisters, she added, " The fog is lifting, and my head feels full of cotton wool instead of ideas for books. So who will come for a scramble on the rocks with me this afternoon ? "

# CHAPTER IV

## SHOPPING—BUT NOT IN BOND STREET

"HALLO!" cried Vivien as Jill came running downstairs to breakfast a few days later. "Pam wants me to go to the town for her. Would you like to come along?"

Would Jill? Rather! So when the meal was over Miss Merrick produced her list, and Vivien read it aloud, while Jill peeped over her shoulder.

"*Lump sugar, soap flakes, sardines, a pot of blacking and a brush, currants, two large bottles of ink.* We do get through that, darling, don't we? *Bacon, rice, matches, curtain rings, and oranges.* Pam, dear, you do scribble," expostulated Vivien.

Jill began to giggle helplessly.

"We're so used to it!" laughed Miss Merrick. "Good luck. Don't upset the blacking or I shan't love you any more."

Vivien made-believe to kneel at her feet and vow her utmost care; then, tossing her curly bob back from her face she jumped up. "Get your things on, kid, while I start Eric," she cried as she snatched her red beret and her old tweed coat off the hall-stand, and was out of the front door and round to the shed before Jill could blink.

" Sprite ! " thought Miss Merrick. " What a child Vivien is for seventeen. And the dearest, truest chum I've ever had."

This morning the car was cold, and consequently stubborn, so Jill was ready long before Vivien had coaxed it into life. " This starting-handle is a bore ! " she grumbled, chucking it on to the back seat when at last satisfactory noises came from the engine.

" Don't you ever lose it ? " asked Jill.

" I did once, and we were hung up for ages." Vivien slipped into the driver's seat. " I ought to be more careful, for it would be the easiest thing in the world to snatch," she added, steering Eric out into the lane.

Jill turned to look back as they ground up the long curly hill. The sea was blue, and green, and mauve, changing colour every minute as the scudding clouds cast their shadows upon it, while the gulls looked like dots of white as they wheeled and soared, screaming, over the bay. White horses, whipped by the keen March wind, were tumbling round the base of the headland, and sweeping up far across the sands.

Jill suddenly felt glad as she had never been glad in all her life before. The whole world seemed to have become alive ; even the distant hills did not seem so brown and bare.

" It's the spring," said Vivien, as if she guessed her thought. " Don't you love the smell of wet earth, and growing things, and the sea ? "

And Jill, wrinkling up her nose like a rabbit, poked her head out over the side of the car and sniffed as if she would breathe in all the spring at once.

" I say, Vivien, do be a sport and let me drive the car," she said, after a while. " It looks as easy as winking and I'd love to have a shot at it."

" No, you're not old enough," said Vivien tactlessly.

Jill's cheeks flamed. " I think you are too jolly bossy for anything," she exploded. " So there ! "

" Your opinion of me doesn't matter a rap ! " Vivien flashed back, with something in her tone that squashed Jill. " But cars are not to be played with, and the sooner you get that into your head the better."

" Oh, have it your own way. I was only ragging," Jill muttered. " Yes, I promise I'll leave the driving to you, so don't get ratty." But as she spoke Jill grinned her mischievous curly grin, for there were lots of things she could do to Eric without getting into the driver's seat even, and, after all, Vivien was not a proper grown-up to be giving orders like that. It would serve her jolly well right to be taken down a peg.

Round the next bend they nearly ran into the carrier, nodding drowsily as he ambled along. The tumble-down cart, pasted all over with notices of bygone fairs, was stuffed with bags and bundles, and on the back axle swung the old roan's nose-bag.

" Old Thomas is a good sort," said Vivien as the bitter smell of his bad tobacco drifted after them on the wind, " but he must hug the middle of the road, and he could not go any quicker to save his life ! "

" Vivien ! " gasped Jill, for the truth had dawned upon her. " You don't mean that is the carrier ! You were a brick to keep my trunk out of his clutches. And yet I thought Jim was slow."

" That was because you had never met any one who was really slow," answered Vivien, driving on fast now that she had a clear road.

At last, at the foot of the long slope before them they saw a cluster of houses huddled round a great grey church. Vivien pointed. " That is Saint Pennah. And what they don't stock we have to go without, unless we go to the fag of driving into Penzance."

It was mid-morning, and a hush was over the

place; the signboard of the Blue Boar Inn creaked softly as it swung in the breeze, and five white ducks quacked as they waddled up from the road under the churchyard wall.

Vivien braked outside a shop where jars of variegated sweets, pink glass vases, and picture post cards filled up the jutting bow-window.

Jill followed her through the door, and a friendly hen clucked in after them. The shop, though crammed from floor to ceiling with a medley of goods, was deserted.

Vivien scuffled with her feet, then, growing tired of waiting, she cried, " Hi! Mrs. Polgrain ! "

" 'Ere I be, missie. I was just a-cleaning of myself," explained a stout, round-about little soul, as she came scurrying out of a door at the back. Smoothing her apron, she dodged behind the counter and asked, " What can I do for you to-day ? "

Jill mouched out into the sunshine again, and looked about her idly. An old lady and a fat black cat had come out to bask in the sunshine, and two cronies, leaning on their broom handles, gossiped across a fence. There was absolutely nothing doing in Saint Pennah, thought Jill ; she might just as well go and sit in the car and wait for Vivien.

As she opened the door the starting-handle

caught her eye. Like a flash Vivien's words came back to her. " It would be the easiest thing in the world to snatch, and I'd be hung up for ages."

Jill looked quickly about her. The gossips had gone back to their cottages, and there was no one in sight. It was now or never, and she jolly well meant to pay Vivien out for being so bossy.

Leaning over the side of the car Jill grabbed the starter, and ran away up the street at top speed with it.

Meanwhile Vivien and the shopkeeper took their time in going through Miss Merrick's list. Presently, leaving Mrs. Polgrain to tie up the parcels, Vivien went to get the blacking, curtain rings, and ink, which were out of stock, at the other general shop a few doors up the street.

She blinked as she came out into the bright sunshine. " I say, Jill—where are you ? " she cried.

There was no answer.

" Oh well, she can't be far," thought Vivien. " I'll just go and get the rest of the things ! Oh, bother, wherever is my starting-handle ! " she exclaimed, as she fumbled wildly in the back of the car. " I thought I knew just where I had put it."

Suddenly she realized what had happened.

" Jill has run away with it to get even with me about the driving. Oh, what a little ijjut."

The church clock struck twelve, and the children who were gathered in the playground of the school poured out through the gates like a torrent in spate.

" I know what I'll do ! " cried Vivien. Turning in a flash she dashed back into the shop, flung down sixpence, snatched up a big bag of bulls' eyes, and was out into the street again before Mrs. Polgrain could do more than gasp. She ran to the mounting block outside the Blue Boar Inn, and jumped up on it. " Hi, kiddies ! " she shouted, clapping her hands to attract their attention. " I've lost some one, and I want you all to help me to find her. She isn't grown up, and she has curly red hair. She can't be far, either, because I've only just missed her. So who wants to earn some bulls' eyes ? "

For a second they stared in bewilderment, some sucking their thumbs ; then, crying, " Coo, let's find Carrots and get some sweets," they scattered in all directions, shouting at the top of their voices.

" Set a kid to catch a kid," laughed Vivien. She stood by the car, looking up and down the street, but she had not long to wait.

" Oh, there's Carrots. Carrots ! " a babel of voices soon rose excitedly, and clutching the

"*I've lost some one, and I want you all to help me to find her.*"

bag of sweets, Vivien sprinted towards the noise.
And there, round the very next corner was the
carrier's cart, surrounded by the shouting mob
of excited children.

"Oh! Oh! Carrots!" they shrilled.
"There's your Carrots! We've found her."
About three dozen grubby forefingers pointed
at Jill, whose cheeks were as red as her hair
as she sat huddled on the box-seat beside old
Thomas.

"Vivien!" she stammered out. "I only did
it for a rag! Take your old starting-handle—
and call your pack off."

"Thank you, children, you've done very well,"
said Vivien, smiling mischievously at Jill over the
tops of their heads as they crowded round her
for the reward she shared out among them.

Sucking loudly, they all trooped off at last,
and Jill, beside herself, climbed down from the
cart and thrust the starting-handle into Vivien's
hands. Old Thomas was laughing openly,
which did not improve Jill's temper, as he
touched his cap to Vivien, and whipping up his
horse, he disappeared round the corner.

Jill gritted her teeth as she followed Vivien
up the street. "No one—no one—no one," she
muttered to herself, "shall call me Carrots
again."

"What's the murmuration?" Vivien turned,

with an exasperating lift of her eyebrows. " I'm
sorry, Jill, but you brought it on yourself, you
know, by playing such a kiddish trick. The best
thing was to get some other kids to deal with it
for me ; it seemed more in their line."

" It isn't that ; it's what they called me."
Jill stamped her foot. " I don't care about anything else."

" I'm sorry," Vivien turned to her frankly.
" I never thought they would yell like that.
They were little hooligans to get personal."

But Jill would not be appeased, and it was with
a scowling face that she stumped after Vivien
to Mrs. Polgrain's. While the older girl was
settling up the bill, Jill poked round among the
jumble of things on the counter. Suddenly she
saw a small black bottle. Idly she turned it over
and read the label. Jill's attention was roused at
once. What did it say ? As used by nobility,
society, and the stage ! Why, it was too good to
be true. She must buy it even if it cost her all
her money. No one should call her Carrots
again.

And while Vivien had her back turned, stowing
the bulky parcels into the car, Jill, fumbling
frantically in her purse, fished out the price of
the bottle of hair dye. It took all her money but
threepence, but she did not care. Slipping her
prize into the deep pocket of her coat, she

managed to look quite unconcerned when Vivien called her.

"Jill, I'm going to get Pam some chocolates. How much can you run to?"

Jill flushed like a peony. She had never thought of this. She rooted wildly in her pocket, but no counting would make those three wretched pennies any more.

At last, shamefaced, she held them out.

Vivien looked puzzled. "Thanks," she said, and turned away to choose some chocolates, the very nicest she could find, and then the girls scrambled back into the car.

The bottle dug into Jill's side as she huddled herself up among the parcels on the back seat. "Never mind, I won't care if I did seem mean just now," she thought to herself. "I can't say what I gave all my money for, but they'll soon see."

# CHAPTER V

" I SAY, Jill, I wish you would let me paint your portrait ! " cried Vivien one afternoon when the rain was dashing on the window with a sound like hail, and there could be no going out. Miss Merrick, directly after lunch, had taken a pile of printer's proofs into the study, leaving the girls in the sitting-room at a loose end.

" Paint me ? " cried Jill, puzzled, for she had thought that only really beautiful girls had their portraits done. " You're pulling my leg ! Who would want to draw my ginger mop and freckled nose ? "

" No, I mean it," answered Vivien. " Sit there on the window seat. Oh yes, you can write to Lambie, as you call her, if you like. But you must lean forward so that the light just catches your cheek. Excuse my fiddling with your hair," continued Vivien, as Jill settled herself obediently, " but I want it fluffed out like a sort of halo."

" Halo ! " giggled Jill. " I don't think."

*" Excuse my fiddling with your hair."*

"Now, that's splendid. Keep just as you are!" Vivien cried with a rapt look on her face as she turned away to rummage in the cupboard for her drawing-board and paint-box.

It was very quiet in the room ; some coal fell out of the grate with a clatter ; the wind sang round the corners of the house, rising sometimes to a little shriek ; the window pane against which Jill leant was all diamonded with rain, and the roar of the returning tide suddenly sounded horribly near.

"Where did you learn to draw?" asked Jill presently.

"Daddy taught me all I know," Vivien answered softly. "I was eight years old when Mother died, and Daddy could not bear to stay in any place that reminded him of her being ill, so we went away from Cornwall to the south of France. Besides," she added sadly, "Daddy had never got well after the war. He craved the sun, I think. We lived for a whole year in a little white villa by the Mediterranean. There are no tides there, so we were almost at the edge of the waves, and it didn't matter."

"It's like a fairy tale!" cried Jill, as she finished her letter and screwed the cap on her fountain-pen, in the hope of getting Vivien to tell her some more.

"We had a tangled, overgrown garden with a

fountain in it that never played," went on Vivien dreamily, as she sketched. "There were lots of palm trees, too, and yuccas, oleanders, azaleas, and things, all flowering wild. Oh, if you've once seen the colour out there you can't forget it! The blue of the sea, like the sapphires in Mother's ring; the grey olive trees, and the snow mountains, white against the sky."

Jill, forgetting that she was supposed to keep still, turned to look at Vivien. "How you do love colour," she said.

Vivien, forgetting the picture too, stared straight before her with eyes that saw nothing. "If I had my way," she said, "I would live in a studio, on dry bread if I could not run to butter, and paint like Daddy." She went on, half to herself, "I dream of it all sometimes still, and wake up fancying that I can smell the mimosa. And I can see the oranges growing on the trees like little balls of fire whenever I shut my eyes. This house of Pam's is home, she has made it that; but the south is fairyland. And I want, oh, how I want to go back!"

And then there came a rattle of crockery outside, and Jill, moving stiffly, said, "It can't be tea-time yet!"

"It's all of that, miss." Cook set the laden tray on the table as Miss Merrick put her head round the study door.

" Who said tea ?　Magic word ! " she cried.
Then crossing the room, Auntie Pam leaned over
Vivien's shoulder to look at the little picture to
which the girl was just putting the finishing
touches.

" Oh, it is good ! " cried Miss Merrick, seeing
how Vivien had brought out the coppery lights
in Jill's hair, the girl's one beauty if she had only
known it, while in the background a faded curtain
draped a window all wet with rain.

" Do you like it, Pam dear ! "　Vivien
nuzzled her head against her shoulder like a
friendly pony.　" Have it, to keep," she said.

And Miss Merrick, laying down the portrait
to kiss the girl, said softly, " I wonder, darling,
if you realize the value of the work you give me
with both hands."

Clatter !　Flop !　Bang ! went the letter-box,
and Jill jumped up and came running back again
with a square white envelope in her hand.
" You're the lucky one to-day, Auntie," she said.

Miss Merrick gave a startled gasp.　Her hand
shook a little as she turned the envelope over and
stared at it.　She knew that handwriting well,
though she had never thought, somehow, to see
it again.

Vivien looked troubled.　" That letter has
given Pam a real shake up," she thought.　" I
wonder what it means."

But Miss Merrick did not say anything, only slipped it into the pocket of her jumper, and poured out tea for them with a bright colour in her cheeks and a rather forced gaiety.

It was cut and come again at the big brown loaf, and the dish of thick yellow cream had something magic about it, Jill thought, for however much every one ate, there still seemed to be enough.

Then they played charades, and the dressing up ended in a frolic all over the house, shrieking with laughter at absurd jokes, till the grandfather clock in the hall chimed nine booming strokes, and Miss Merrick shooed the girls upstairs to bed.

As the door closed behind them Miss Merrick sat down by the fire and took the letter from her pocket. Her face was very thoughtful as she read the closely written pages through slowly, dwelling on each word. Squibb came and sat at her feet, as if he understood, and nudged his cold nose into her hand for sympathy. Every loop and twirl of the writing reminded her of her music-student days in London, when she had a home behind her, and worked and wrote for the fun of being on her own, and not because she had to, which made all the difference.

In all the memories of that time was Keith Middleton. And when he heard he had won a scholarship that meant three years in Rome she had been the first he had told. They had celebrated together. Fame had seemed within his grasp then, and her eyes were starry.

But that wonderful evening had been the last time of all, for his letters, thick as autumn leaves at first, had grown fewer, till they ceased altogether.

Then her father's business had crashed, and six months after he had died, a beaten man. The old home had been sold, and she had had to turn out and buckle to, somehow, anyhow, to make ends meet and help pay the debts.

Keith Middleton had never written after that ; never until to-day.

A particularly loud bump overhead brought Miss Merrick's thoughts back to the present with a jerk. Jill and Vivien were evidently brightening up undressing by a pillow fight, to judge by the squeals of laughter.

Presently all was quiet upstairs, and then Vivien, in her old red dressing-gown, crept in. " Did I disturb you ? " she whispered, seeing Miss Merrick start. " I left my book. . . ."

" No, come in and sit down ! " answered Pamela Merrick, beckoning the girl to her favourite perch on the humpty before the fire. " I've had a letter to-day from an old friend, Keith Middleton." A bright patch of colour rose in her cheeks. " I can't realize him as successful," she added.

" The Keith Middleton ! " Vivien looked up into her face, wide-eyed with astonishment. " You don't mean the painter ? "

" Yes, we met when he was at the Slade, and I was studying music. I was only a little older than you are now, and he was twenty-three, with all his way to make."

" It's a sin you've let your music drop," said Vivien.

" I had no choice," Miss Merrick answered. " I was never good enough with my violin to earn a living."

" Yes, earn ! " snorted Vivien. " Nothing seems any good if you can't earn money by it ! Look at my paintings. All my luck, except just finding you, has been right out since Daddy died."

Her rebellious little face was in the shadow, but the hands she stretched out to the blaze shook a little. Miss Merrick gently touched her rumpled mop of hair. " Don't talk like that, Vivien. I can't bear to hear you. People will discover Martin Trevone one day—and he will be the artist of our time."

" When I am ' old and grey and full of sleep,' huddled over a handful of coals in a bed-sitter," answered Vivien bitterly.

" I wish I could help you, kiddie, but my hands

are tied. C.A., as you call it. I'm a selfish woman, though, for I'm glad we met."

" Glad is not the word for what I feel," replied Vivien, slipping off the humpty to kneel upon the rug, with her head resting on Miss Merrick's knees. " I would rather live with you here than I would with the Queen," she said a trifle tremulously.

" Go to bed," exclaimed Miss Merrick, with her own eyes misty. " It is late enough for little girls." Then, in the voice that showed she was tired and a little sad, " Give me a good kiss before you go."

Vivien put her arms round her neck and hugged her, then stole upstairs. As the door closed softly Miss Merrick got up and went across to the window. She pulled back the curtain and leaned her forehead against the pane. " How I would like to be going to a theatre to-night," she thought, suddenly craving to hear the London traffic slurring through the wet ; to see the electric signs blazing overhead, and to have the shuffling feet of the crowds in her ears again, instead of this everlasting sea.

She turned back to the table and turned the oil-lamp higher. " How it smells ! " she said to herself disgustedly, as she fetched her pen and the ink. " Yes, I'll write to Keith to-night and ask him to help Vivien for the sake of the days

when he was eating his own heart out for success.
It is always easier to ask favours for some one
else," she added.

And there was silence in the little room,
except for the snoring of Squibb and the whisper
and rustle of the driftwood fire, burning with a
blue, ghostly flame on the hearth.

But it was not an easy letter to write after all.
It is never a simple matter to pick up the dropped
threads of a friendship. Miss Merrick paused
at last, chewing the end of her pen like a school-
girl.

" I wonder if Keith is married ? " she thought.
" He can't be, though, or I would have heard.
But he is engaged, probably. Now Keith has
made his name he must have all the society
lovelies at his feet. I wonder if it has ruined
him, or if he has kept his merry laugh."

And she bent again over her letter, and wrote
quickly, pleading for Vivien's gift till the fire
died down, and it grew cold.

# CHAPTER VI

## " THEY SHAN'T CALL ME CARROTS ! "

ALL this time the black bottle that Jill had smuggled in with her from the shopping expedition lay safely hidden under a pile of woollies at the back of her drawer, and she was simply dying to try its effect upon her hair.

" Carrots, indeed ! " Jill muttered every time she saw herself in the glass. " No one shall call me Carrots again."

And then, just as Jill was beginning to wonder if she would ever get the house to herself, Auntie Pam, tired and inky after a hard morning's writing, came into the sitting-room and suggested their going primrosing.

" Primroses ? How lovely ! " cried Vivien, looking up from her detested mending. " Pam, put my name down."

Jill was just opening her mouth to jump at the idea too, when, like a flash, she remembered that it was Cook's afternoon out. So it was now or never for her experiment. She resolved to feign interest in the detective story she was reading, and get herself left behind.

" What about you, Jill ? " smiled her aunt, but Jill hunched herself over her book and grunted an unintelligible answer.

" Wake up ! " Vivien spoke to the top of her bent head. " Is that grunt for yes or no ? "

Jill shrugged her shoulders with well-acted impatience. " Have I got to go, Auntie ? " she drawled.

" No, of course not," replied Aunt Pamela, puzzled. " I thought you would like to, that's all."

" Oh, let me read ! " snapped Jill, and Miss Merrick turned away. Vivien's eyebrows lifted slightly. " Fancy wanting to fug indoors on a day like this ! " she said scornfully as she closed the door behind her.

Jill's heart thumped, but she had the sense to sit where she was, with her head bent down over the page she had forgotten to turn. She listened hard. Yes, they were coming downstairs now, laughing and calling for Squibby. " Bye, bye, Jill ! " they cried ; then the hall door shut noisily, and they were gone.

Jill ran upstairs to the landing-window that looked out up the valley. She peeped out cautiously from behind the curtains. Auntie Pam and Vivien, with baskets on their arms, and Squibb lolloping in front of them, were going down towards the marsh. As their happy voices came back to her on the light breeze, the girl felt like craning out and shouting to them to wait for her. But she fought the impulse, and said to herself, " Now is my chance. And I'll do it as soon as Cook is out of the house."

The next few minutes seemed ages to Jill's impatience. She was even beginning to wonder if Cook had washed up like lightning and got out already, when she heard a distant door bang. Then Cook, in a tight new blue coat, hurried down the path to the gate wheeling her bicycle. Swiftly Jill ducked below the level of the sill. Holding her breath, she listened for the faint click of the closing gate.

" Now for it ! No more red hair for me," thought Jill as she tiptoed, though there was absolutely no one to hear, across the landing and in at her bedroom door.

Meanwhile, Aunt Pamela and Vivien made their way down the slope towards the rushing brown stream. They scrambled through a gap in the hedge, and then picked their way through the long tangled grass of the marsh, with black mud beneath, into which their feet sank with a squedgy sound. They followed up the stream until they came to a little copse of hazel bushes, alders, and one or two stunted oaks. As she pushed through the low neglected hedge Vivien gave a cry of pleasure, for all the ground, except for patches of moss and the drifted leaves of last year, was covered with primroses. The pale spring sunshine glinted through the interlacing twigs on to the gold at their feet and the rippling water of the brook.

"Oh, the darlings," whispered Miss Merrick as she settled down to pick, and when she rose to her feet at last, with her hands wet with leaves, she pressed the bunch she had gathered to her face and kissed it, as if the primroses were alive as a person is alive.

Vivien, her hands full of palm, paused and watched, all her quick sense of beauty stirred. "How I would like to paint Pam as she looks this minute," the girl thought, longing so much that it hurt for proper lessons, a studio where she could mess about undisturbed, and, above all, to have her father beside her again, now encouraging, now ruthlessly pointing out a fault ; but all the time understanding as no one else had ever understood.

Miss Merrick, all unconscious, broke the spell. "I wonder what Squibb has got there?" she cried. Next minute his furry paws began to fly, and to her horror Miss Merrick saw he was digging up a very ancient bone. "Strong

*She pressed the bunch she had gathered to her face and kissed it.*

measures will have to be taken, old chap, if you
bring that home," she laughed.

The sun went in, and it grew very grey and

cold in the copse. They turned towards home. Vivien, looking over her shoulder now and then, had to giggle to see Squibby trailing along behind with his find, from which he had growlingly refused to part, sticking out on either side of his jaws like the tusks of a walrus.

" I'll shut him in the woodshed ! " said Miss Merrick, laying hold of his collar as they approached the house. " So go on ahead, darling."

" Coo-ee, Jill ! " called Vivien as she opened the hall door. " You were a goose not to come."

No answer.

Not a sound but the rustle of the incoming tide and the ticking of the grandfather clock in the echoing, suddenly eerie house.

" Where are you, Jill ? " cried Vivien, as she ran across the hall, looked first in the dining-room, and then peeped into the study, but Jill was nowhere downstairs.

" How awfully queer ! " she thought as she stood still and listened. There came a sound of footsteps moving about in the bedroom overhead, and then the crash of something falling. " Whatever is she doing ? " said Vivien, feeling more than a little alarmed. She ran upstairs crying, " What's the matter ? "

There was no reply, so she knocked loudly on Jill's bedroom door, and called, " Come out and tell me what's happened ? "

" I won't ! " A queer muffled voice that was unmistakably Jill's shouted through the key-hole. " Not unless you promise not to rag me."

" Don't be an owl," retorted Vivien. " Let me in ! " She stretched out her hand for the door handle, but it was locked. " Jill, this is a bit too thick ! " she exclaimed quite crossly. " What are you trying to spring on Pam and me ? "

" This ! " The door was suddenly jerked open from inside, and Vivien saw that the washstand was in a fearful pickle, and that a black bottle, overturned, oozed on to the floor. And then she had no eyes for anything, for Jill, with scarlet cheeks and a defiant expression on her face, burst out on to the landing and faced her. " There— now you know ! " she said.

" B-but your—hair ! " Astonishment jerked the words from Vivien. " It's gone—green ! "

" What's the matter, girls ? " called Miss Merrick anxiously from the foot of the stairs.

" Pam ! " Vivien shouted back. " Just come and look ! Of all the weird kids ! "

Auntie Pam rushed upstairs. " She has tried to dye her hair ! " she cried the instant she saw Jill. " Oh, what a shame ! It was such a glorious, coppery red."

" And if I did want to change it, candidly, I wouldn't choose green," put in Vivien.

" Some dyes, if they are not handled very expertly, do turn hair a sort of green," explained Miss Merrick, lifting a strand of it in her fingers sadly. Jill's hair was certainly a weird colour, more like a dull bronze-green than anything else, with here and there a streak of its own red coming through.

" Suppose you tell me all about it ? " coaxed Auntie Pam at last.

And out the story came, from the moment Jill had seen the bottle of hair dye in the village shop, till this afternoon when she contrived to be left behind to carry out her plan in peace.

" I saw my hair was a fearful mess even while it was wet ! " Jill burst out. " But I dried it at the sitting-room fire, and hoped it would look better. But it looked much, much worse. And when I heard you and Vivien at the gate I bolted up here," she ended bitterly.

" Well, the first thing to do is to wash it," said her aunt practically. " Cook is out, so I'll put some water on to heat."

Auntie Pam soon had two kettles singing merrily on the stove ; then she called Jill down, and for a whole weary hour she scrubbed, and soaped, and rubbed, and rinsed. Presently Vivien, with a perfectly grave face, came out of her room, for she had run away to get her laugh

*For a whole weary hour she scrubbed, and soaped, and rubbed, and rinsed.*

over. Now she joined in with a will, but the case was hopeless ; they might all as well have been scouring the original red.

"This is a fast dye all right," cried Vivien at

last, as she straightened up to ease her aching back. "Pam, what are we to do?"

"Oh, please let me rest for a minute," groaned poor Jill. "My head is simply splitting."

"But she can't stay all her life with green hair!" said Vivien, and Jill, appalled at the prospect, looked as if she was going to cry.

"Don't be silly! Of course she is not going to do that. I know!" Miss Merrick exclaimed after a pause. "I will dry it off quickly at the sitting-room fire, if you, Vivien, will bring her in a cup of tea. Then Jill shall go to bed before Cook comes in. A bad headache like this is excuse enough. And in the morning Jill and I and Eric will run over and spend the day in Penzance, where nobody knows us, and see what a good hairdresser can suggest? How about that, dears?"

"Topping!" exclaimed Vivien, sitting down thankfully on the edge of the kitchen table. "You are a genius, Pam."

But she thought jealously, "I wonder if she would give up a day's work for me?" And then, with a shiver, came the remembrance of those black days after her father died—for Pam was all she had now.

Jill could not say out loud, "Thank you, Auntie darling, for thinking of my feelings so"; but she meant it with all her heart as she drank her tea thirstily, and realized that her crazy prank had made things worse than before.

" I wish to goodness I *were* Carrots now ! " she said bitterly.

# CHAPTER VII

## THE CAIRN ON THE MOOR

JILL came back from Penzance with her hair cropped off amazingly short, and though she smeared pomade on it whenever she remembered, to make it grow quicker, the boyish effect suited her well enough, and her disastrous escapade was soon forgotten.

She had quite settled down in the little white house on the sands, and she felt as if she had known Vivien all her life. The girls and Squibb had many rambles over the countryside on these lengthening spring days, but Vivien was often busy typewriting or helping Aunt Pamela with literary work, and then Jill, left at a loose end, got out her lesson books and tried to revise her old examination papers. But it seemed a hopeless task, and her dream of going to Beechdene faded a little, and, after all, there were plenty of new interests to fill her time.

" I say, Vivien, let's go and see the funny old cairn you pointed out to me the day I came ! " cried Jill one morning when work was slack.

" What a good idea ! " answered Vivien. " It's a long climb, but if you're game I am." And she ran out to the kitchen to ask Cook for a picnic lunch.

Jill felt a little thrill of anticipation as she tugged on her brogues, for she hoped, perhaps, to get Vivien to tell her some more. The older girl fascinated Jill, for she was willing to talk so much, but not of the one thing that piqued Jill's curiosity—how and why, after all her wandering, she had come to be the youngest secretary-companion in the world.

" Hi ! " Jill shouted presently. " I'm ready ! "

But Vivien was " whirling," as she called it, round a terribly untidy room, for she could not find one shoe, and was wild about it.

" I say, hurry up ! " cried Jill as she peeped in at the door.

" I *am* hurrying. Oh, go away, do ! "

So Jill clattered down the stairs calling for Squibby. She found him, looking more like an old rug than ever, curled up on Auntie's pet bulbs in the sheltered bed under the sitting-room window.

" Squibb ! How can you ? " she reproached him. A brown eye opened sleepily, then, realizing that she had a hat on, Squibb uncurled himself like lightning and pounded down the path to the gate.

At last Vivien came downstairs. " I've got it ! " she cried.

" Where was it ? " asked Jill mischievously.

" Er—in the shoe box. I never thought of looking there."

Vivien slung the satchel with the picnic lunch across her shoulders, and calling good-bye to Cook, the girls banged the white gate after them.

Clouds scudded across the sky, but there was enough blue to make a Dutchman a pair of trousers, as Vivien said. The dead leaves that had clung to the branches all the winter were being torn off now, and Vivien jumped and clutched at them as if she were seven instead of seventeen.

" It's lucky to grab a falling leaf," she cried, " and I do want Pam to have luck with her new book."

" What's it about ? " asked Jill, when Vivien paused for breath. " Is it crooks, as usual ? "

Vivien smiled, then her face grew grave. " It is quite different from anything Pam has done before," she said. " There are no hairbreadth escapes, but it is so awfully true to life. The girl is a music student on her own in town, as Pam used to be, and the man is some one she has met, I'm sure. He is too alive to be just a made-up person. You can see everything in your head as you read it. Pam has got more than just a gift for writing."

The girls followed the cart-track up the valley, past the primrose copse; crossed a narrow plank-bridge over the rushing brown stream and came out on open moorland that stretched up to the very sky. Great masses of cloud were piled up all round, and every now and then a puff of wind fanned their cheeks.

Then suddenly it seemed the slope grew easier, and they were on the crest of the hill. Jill, draw-ing long breaths of the keen salt air, cried de-lightedly, "The view is worth all that climb."

Away all round stretched the browny-grey masses of the heather, then, as the land sloped down, the girls saw their own valley with the little white house standing on the very edge of the sands, and beyond it a tumbling yeasty sea.

To the girls' right stretched another valley and another bay. Vivien kissed her hand to a square grey house that looked deceptively near. "That is Dr. Grant's," she explained. "He and his wife are perfect dears. It's lucky, though, that we are none of us ever ill, for it would be such an awful way to go and fetch him. We've no phone—C.A. again, of course. Oh, it's so fresh up here I want to sprint," she cried as she dashed away. Jill sprang after her, and with Squibb scampering along at their heels they raced towards the cairn that loomed up in front of them, grey above the withered grass, under the pale watery sky.

Jill felt suddenly that wild horses would not drag her here in the twilight. " Who built it ? " she asked when Vivien checked her pace.

" No one knows ! Some people think the Piskies lent a hand. They say unearthly lights glow above these stones, and that on stormy nights you hear the ring of a horse's hooves, as if he were galloping hard, and shrieks . . ."

Vivien broke off abruptly, for Jill, shuddering, had put her fingers in her ears. " Uncork, old thing ! " cried Vivien. " It's only a tale ! "

Hooking her arm through the younger girl's she drew her away. But Jill, fascinated still, looked back to see again the hoary mound of stone, dun grey under the lowering sky.

It was later than either realized, and the girls suddenly discovered that they were ravenous, so they huddled themselves under the lee of a boulder that jutted out from the moor side. It made a tiny cave, sheltering them from the rising wind that whistled over the heather with a little creepy sound that set Jill's teeth on edge.

Vivien unslung the satchel, and Squibb, smelling the food almost before they had decided to unwrap it, came and sprawled between their feet and whined. At last, disgruntled because they insisted on keeping some for themselves, he wandered off after his own affairs.

" Wouldn't it be glorious if I could win the Faith Anderson scholarship and get to Beechdene that way ! " remarked Jill, and Vivien shivered, and said jerkily, " Don't talk about it."

There was a little pause, and then Vivien went on in a queer little broken voice, " Pam says I must try not to mind so about Daddy. She thinks I ought to be proud. And so I am ; but I can see that shimmering, treacherous Mediterranean sea, and Daddy and I bathing, as clearly as if it had happened yesterday."

Jill, holding a bar of chocolate in one hand, crooked the other sympathetically across Vivien's shoulders, but she could not think of anything to say.

" It is so lovely and warm there in the south," went on Vivien, giving Jill's hand a little grateful squeeze, " that you can stay in for hours, but you see, Daddy never swam really well because of his war wound. He was always ill, more or less."

Jill's eyes were misty. " Oh, poor dear," she whispered.

" Well, that day I had been frolicking in the shallows with him ; then I went in to dress, and boil up the hot drink I always had ready for him when he came out. Foreigners' tea isn't like ours a bit, and Daddy loathed it, so I had a wee stove. I just slipped on a beach suit, it was so gloriously warm that one did not want to wear many clothes, and then I tried to get the kettle to boil. But the stove was all cussed, and would not heat. All the time I was thinking, ' If I'm not quick perhaps Daddy will get another chill,' when suddenly I heard a lot of shouting, and our name —Daddy's and mine."

Jill's fingers tightened on the hand she held. She guessed what was coming, and she felt more sorry for Vivien than she ever had done for any one in all her life.

" I rushed down the beach toward a little crowd that had gathered at the water's edge, but they would not let me through," went on Vivien in a toneless, dreary voice, staring straight before her with eyes that saw nothing. " A kind ice-cream woman put her arms round me, and I remember thinking that I had got into a queer sort of bad dream, with the only real thing in it the smell of garlic in her breath as she bent over me. And then, presently, they told me that another man had got into difficulties far out in the current round the outer rocks. And my darling Daddy, who was just a smashed up wreck of war, heard the cry for help. And he never waited for any one else to go, but plunged in himself, and brought the other man on shore. But it killed him, Jill, that dreadful long swim against the current, supporting some one else. I know I ought to be proud ! " Vivien went on brokenly, " I am—really ! But I miss my Daddy so."

Jill shivered. This was the most pitiful tale she had ever listened to. One read of tragedies in books, but she had never thought of things happening to any one she knew—to a girl only three years older than herself. No wonder Vivien had said, " People who do the rescuing don't always get well like Faith Anderson ! "

" And so they buried him in the little grave-yard on the cliff top above the sea that killed him. And I was left to get on with things."

Vivien broke off, and stared out over a heaving grey sea, where the sun was going down like a ball of fire into a bank of clouds and fog.

# CHAPTER VIII

## ON THE MOORS IN THE DUSK

VIVIEN and Jill, in their cubby-hole under the boulder, were so deep in talk that the time passed like a flash, and the light began to change as the sun dipped below the surface of the sea.

Vivien roused herself at last. " Ow ! I'm stiff ! " she exclaimed. She peeped at her watch, and, with a gasp of horror, she jumped up. " My hat ! it's nearly six ! And we're miles from home ! " she cried.

Jill scrambled out from under the boulder. The rising wind seemed to cut to the bone. " I wish we hadn't got to go past that beastly cairn," she thought.

Slipping, sliding, and taking short runs now and then, the girls made their way down the moor side as quickly as they could. Vivien, glancing at the black clouds that were driving across the last of the sunset, and hoping to shorten the distance, left the winding stony track, and plunged straight across the deep heather.

Too late to turn back she realized her mistake,

for it was now impossible to make any pace at all. Rabbit-holes honeycombed the ground ; brambles wound themselves about their shins ; pebbles started from beneath their feet and rattled till Jill fancied that something was at her heels.

The hills were blotted out by the gathering gloom ; the ragged gorse bushes were already ominous shapes behind which simply anything might be lurking. Far away across the valley there twinkled a little light. " Don't you wish we were safe at home roasting chestnuts ? " said Vivien, tantalizing herself.

Jill looked back at the cairn that towered above them. The last glint of the setting sun caught the stones till they seemed to glow. The eerie rushing of the wind seemed to come from everywhere at once, and the threshing of the returning tide suddenly sounded horribly cruel. Far away, on the upland fields, the girls heard the long-drawn howls of a sheep-dog.

And then Jill remembered.

" Oh," she gasped, standing stock - still. " Where's Squibb ? "

" Squibb ? " gasped Vivien, appalled. " I don't know ! We must go back ! "

Turning in a flash, she bounded past Jill, and pelted up the path towards that grisly cairn that looked as dark now as the sky above it. " Oh ! "

she thought, agonized, " if I have lost Pam's Squibby ! "

It did not bear thinking of ; no, not if she and Jill stayed out all night. Soon it would be dark, Pam at home would be anxious ; but Vivien would not think of deserting the dog. Fat old Squibb, with his curly coat, and darling, bossy ways ! Never !

Now Vivien had reached the boulder under which they had sat so happily—what ages ago it seemed ! She stood still and made a trumpet of her hands.

" Squibb ! Squibb ! Squibb ! " she called.

Echo flung the words back at her like a voice that mocked.

Panting a little, crashing through the gorse, Jill came racing up the slope. " Keep quiet ! " snapped Vivien, as she dropped on her knees and laid her ear to the ground.

Faintly she heard a muffled, low whining that seemed to come from somewhere under their feet. " Squibb is caught in a rabbit-hole, I think ! " cried Vivien. " Oh, Squibby, if only you could speak and tell us just where you are."

Vivien, calling, and stopping to listen, made little casts round and about. Soon she was sure that in one spot the whining sounded more clearly. " I believe he is caught in that sort of pit place over there," she said, as she ran to the spot. The girls lay down flat in the gorse, careless of scratches, and craned over the pit. It was not very big, but an ominous-looking tunnel seemed to lead off, and they came to the conclusion that Squibb must be down it somewhere.

" Poor old chap ! We'll get you out in a jiffy ! " Jill shouted, and a storm of frantic whining broke out from the depths below.

" That settles it ! " Vivien's face was white and set as she slipped off her heavy coat to leave her arms free. " I'm going down now ! "

" No, you're not ! " contradicted Jill. " Sorry, but I was head of the gym at my old school, and it's up to me ! "

" But I'm half your size," retorted Vivien. " So I can creep through smaller places."

And Jill did not raise any more objections. Vivien let herself slip over the edge. Clinging to the gorse stems with her numbed fingers the girl scrabbled frantically for a hold with her feet. At last her toes found a projection to rest on, and the strain on her aching arms relaxed. Then, hanging by her hands alone, she lowered herself still further, but she could feel no bottom. The pit did not seem to be very deep, but in the darkness it was impossible to be sure.

Vivien set her teeth ; took a chance, and jumped.

Jill, peering down into the gloom of the hole could just distinguish Vivien's red beret as the other girl dropped on hands and knees to enter the tunnel. Frantic whining broke out afresh. Poor Squibb, terrified, was calling for help as plainly as he knew how.

Vivien had her fair share of imagination, and it took a big effort to crawl into the unknown dark. The opening was very narrow. The sides scraped her elbows, and the roof rubbed her head.

Carefully, feeling forward with her hands, she wriggled along. The earthy smell was unbearable. If she had to go much further she felt she couldn't stick it. And then, just as she was beginning to despair, her hands came up against a great rough stone. Baffled, she gave a little sob, " Oh, Squibby ! Where are you ? " she cried.

At the sound of her voice the whining broke out more loudly than ever. It sounded almost in her ear.

" I think the roof has caved in and trapped him ! " she cried.

Now that she understood what had happened, Vivien scrabbled carefully with her hands to loosen the fallen earth at the sides of the chunk of rock. Then, very warily, in case a hasty movement should send the roof of the tunnel crashing down upon them both, Vivien worked her fingers in till she got a grip of the edges of the jagged lump.

Gingerly, with her heart in her mouth, she pulled.

Oh joy, the chunk of rock moved easily, and as it shifted she felt hot breath on her face, and a wet tongue that licked the tips of her fingers.

" Oh, Squibby ! " she cried thankfully. " So you got in after a bunny, and the roof fell down and jammed you in ! And I believe you're quite all right, and not hurt a bit ! " she added, as she felt the dog pressing strongly on the other side of the barrier. " Come along now, let's get out of this ! " she added, as she moved to turn round. " Help ! I can't turn ! " she gasped out. " I'm wedged in ! "

Cold sweat broke out on her forehead. Then Vivien fought her panic down, for she realized if she crept backwards and drew the stone after her, the dog was sure to follow.

So, calling encouragingly to Squibb, and working the chunk of rock along with her hands, she made her way backwards like a crab. Squibb, wagging his tail, came puffing along after her. Luckily he was not hurt, and his relief at being got out was tremendous.

Vivien's palms were cut with the sharp stones ; her stockings were a wreck ; her curls were caked with grit and dirt, and there was still all the moor that stretched between them and home to be crossed, but she did not care, for the job was done. " I'll keep you on a lead, my Squibby ! " she said. " No more of this ! "

And now, thank goodness, she was scrambling out of the hole, and she could stand upright and stretch her aching back. There above her in the thick gloom she could just discern the white patch that was Jill's anxious face.

" Oh, Vivien, you've really got him ! How splendid ! " Jill cried, as she craned over the pit and stretched out her arms.

Bracing herself against the dog's weight, Vivien lifted him from the ground. But she was not very tall, and try as she would she could not heave him high enough to be within reach of Jill's outstretched hands.

Abruptly, gasping for breath, Vivien set the heavy spaniel down and looked up at Jill, white to the lips.

" We're done," she gasped, " if we can't get him out ! "

" Help ! Help ! " their voices rose in chorus as loudly as they could shout, but in their heart of hearts both Vivien and Jill knew that no help could possibly come.

# CHAPTER IX

## AN UNEXPECTED MEETING

"HALLO! Hallo! What's the matter?"
Running feet came crashing through the gorse, and a moment later a tall man, breathing hard, stood beside Jill.

"Help!" Vivien's frightened voice seemed to come almost from beneath his feet. "Give me a pull out, please!" she cried. "I'm stuck!"

"Great Scott! However did you get in there?" The stranger switched on a pocket electric torch and flashed it down. The beam illumined the deep, narrow hole, and Vivien's white face, with a long scratch across the bridge of her nose, as, dazzled in the sudden glare, she stooped and groped for Squibb.

"Our dog got in after rabbits," she explained, looking a wild little figure with her scarlet beret over one eye, her ragged stockings, and bruised hands. Staggering under Squibb's weight, she heaved his fat body up in her arms. "It's too deep—to climb out of the pit—with him!" she gasped out.

"What a lucky thing I heard you!" the man said as he lay full length in the withered gorse and craned over the pit. He got a firm grip of Squibb's fat furry body with his strong hands. "I say, you haven't starved the old chap!" he gasped out between his teeth as he heaved with all his might.

A moment later and Squibb was frisking round Jill's ankles, giving little eager squeaks like an india-rubber dog in his delight.

"Now it is your turn!" exclaimed the tall man, flashing his torch down once more. Vivien stood on tiptoe and laid her cold, gritty hands in his.

He had nice hands, this stranger, big and strong, and not too smooth. The smell of tobacco and tweeds as he leaned over reminded Vivien of her father.

"Why, you are only a featherweight, kiddie," he exclaimed as he swung her up and out of the hole to safety. "What are you two youngsters doing out here at this time of night?"

"I'm not a kid!" Vivien, who was feeling a trifle unnerved, blurted out in a rush. "I'm Miss Merrick's secretary."

"What a bit of luck!" cried their new friend. "I've been looking for her house. Just drove over from St. Ives, and then I was caught by the sunset off the point. Did you see it ? "

" Yes," said Vivien. " It would make a picture if you had one huge splodge of gold right out to sea, and kept the foreground vague, dark lumps that might be heather and gorse—or any-thing—the Old Things lying in wait, perhaps."

" Artistic little thing," thought the stranger. " How well she has got the idea." Smiling en-couragingly, he slipped a hand under her elbow, saying, " I would like you to see the sketch I made. My bus is on the road just over there ! Let me tuck you both in the back. Then if you'll kindly point out the road, I'll have you home in a jiffy," he added, with a friendly grin at Jill as they made their way along the narrow, stony track to where the side-lights of a big car shone like a pair of glow-worms in the dark.

It was a lovely car ; even in the glimmer of the torch Jill could see that. A dazzle of polish and chromium, and when he opened the door there was a heavenly scent of rich leather and Turkish cigarettes. Their new friend helped them both in and clumsily tucked the rug up round them ; then he settled himself in the driver's seat in front. He fiddled with the con-trols a minute, then switched on the great head-lamps, and the dark leaped back.

" All right behind there ? " he asked pleasantly, turning a silver key as he spoke, and the engine purred like a sleepy cat. " If you are not too done it would be a big help if you could shout out to me where we turn. This rotten country looks so different after dark ! " he added as he let in his clutch.

The purr of the engine changed to a roar, and they were off, not bumping, in spite of the pace, but sliding smoothly along the moorland road. The lamps cut through the dark as a knife cuts through cheese. Rabbits scampered away from the dazzling beam, or crouched, trembling, in the grass, their eyes bright in the light that caught them as the car swept past.

" This is a Rolls Bentley Sports, and it must have cost a mint of money ! " thought Vivien as she looked about her. " And he knows Pam, and paints ? Of course, what a complete ass I am ! This must be Keith Middleton ! "

She studied the clean line of the strong shoulders in front of her, saw the short black hair under the old slouch hat, and remembered what she had been able to see of a strong, trustworthy face.

Now they had left the moor behind them, and following Vivien's directions they swung into the lane that wound between high, ragged hedges down to the stream they could hear rushing over the stones somewhere in the deep valley below. Almost silently they slid round the bend by the dead sloe tree, and Jill thought, " I'll hate Eric for ever after this—nasty little rattle-trap ! "

" That light behind the bridge is Miss Merrick's cottage ! " Vivien reared herself up to call out presently, and a moment later the car glided to a stop outside the white gate.

On the instant, as if some one in the hall had been waiting and listening anxiously, the door flew open, and Pamela Merrick ran down the garden path. She put her arms round the girls, too thankful to see them back safe and sound to realize the blaze of head-lamps in the lane.

" Whatever has happened to you ? " she asked, drawing them closer, and kissing their cold cheeks again and again, as if to make sure they were really there. " Come in, quick ! You must be simply starving ! " she cried.

And then Miss Merrick saw the owner of the car, who snatched off his hat and strode up the garden path, to take both her hands in his—he was so pleased to see her. " Pamela ! It's great to see you again ! " he exclaimed.

Laughing a trifle tremulously, she gripped his outstretched fingers hard.

" Oh, Keith, is it really you ? "

"Why not ?   I'm solid enough, aren't I ? "
he grinned, with just the old flash of white teeth
in a face more tanned, surely, than she remembered.   "And what have you been doing
with yourself all this time ? "

"Just jogging along," Miss Merrick answered
sadly.   "Not like you.   Oh, Keith, I'm
glad ! "

"Just luck," he replied shortly, following her
into the tiny hall.   "Great Scott ! " he exclaimed
"where did you get those paintings ?   They're
Spain itself ! "

Two strides, and he was across the hall, his
face alight with interest in the flicker of the oil
lamp as he looked at Vivien's paintings as if he
could not take his eyes off them.

Vivien drew a step nearer.   She could not
believe she was awake, for she had dreamed so
often that a famous artist might see her work, but
never had she imagined praise like this.

"Those pictures belong to this person here ! "
Smiling delightedly, Miss Merrick slipped her
arm through the girl's and drew her forward.   "Vivien takes after her father," she
explained.

He looked down at the girl at his side.   Little
slip of a thing ; pale face ; ordinary brown hair ;
but those eyes, deep greeny-grey, looking up
shyly through long lashes.   Of whom did they

*He looked at Vivien's paintings as if he could not take his
eyes off them.*

remind him? He could not remember; but
Miss Merrick was speaking. "Did you ever
meet Martin Trevone, the landscape painter?"
she asked.

"Yes. I ran into him in town at some dinner
or other. Great fellow in his own line. Tragic
thing, though!"

"He was my Daddy," said Vivien, clenching

her hands till the knuckles showed white. " Oh, don't talk about that, please ! I know I ought to be proud ; but I miss him so ! "

Mr. Middleton's brown eyes were very gentle as he answered, " You have a father to be proud of. I was never fit to clean his brushes ; but I had luck—while he was fighting ill-health all the time."

And for those few words Vivien gave him all her loyalty.

" Some time, Keith, as I said in my letter, I want your opinion on the last thing Vivien has done," smiled Miss Merrick. " But I can hear the kettle boiling, and I'm sure every one is dying for some tea. Hurry girls, and get tidy, while Mr. Middleton and I have a chat about old times."

The girls dashed upstairs and into their respective rooms. Jill slipped on the simple white dress she wore for prize-giving at her old school, gave her cropped hair a hasty dab with a brush, and called herself ready. But when she opened her door and saw Vivien waiting for her on the landing she gave a little gasp of astonishment. The older girl looked quite grown-up this evening, with dainty, high-heeled shoes on her pretty feet and a silk dress all one smother of flat bright flowers. Her mop of curls had been pushed back behind her shell-like ears, and a pair of fine gold earrings glinted in the light of the hall lamp.

Jill was too shy to enjoy her tea very much. The conversation might have been in Greek for all she understood of it, but Vivien hung spell-bound on each word. Now and then she chipped in, and each time the grown-up people answered her as if she were one of themselves.

When every one had finished they settled themselves round the fire. Keith Middleton's tall figure in the sagging old armchair on one side of the hearth, and Miss Merrick opposite, with Vivien perched on the arm, and steadying herself with one elbow crooked round her neck. Jill thought Auntie Pam was a different person to-night ; her thin cheeks were rosy with happiness, and her eyes like stars. As she looked about her Jill realized that the room looked different too, for her portrait was gone from the mantel-piece.

" What are you writing now, Pamela ? " asked Mr. Middleton, pulling out his tobacco pouch and filling his pipe. " Has the book ever matured ? "

Miss Merrick leaned back among the cushions with her cheek resting on her head. " Yes, it has been coming to life for a long time," she answered. " The trouble is I have such reams of pot-boilers to do first."

" That's a pity. I've seen your name sometimes at the head of——"

" The most appalling rubbish ! " she finished
the sentence for him, smiling wryly.

Before shifting his pipe to the other side of his
mouth he said slowly, " No, your work is never
rubbish, Pamela ; but it is a waste of time for
all that. You—doing crook yarns ! " He flung
back his dark head and laughed, then added
irrelevantly, " You're never in town now, I
suppose ? "

Auntie Pam shook her head, saying, " Almost
never.   The fare is such a frantic price from here."

Her old friend winced. It hurt him to hear
Pamela Merrick speak like that. It seemed all
wrong, somehow, that he should have so much—
a villa on the Riviera, a flat in town, and the
Rolls Bentley Sports ! He looked round at the
shabby room. The cheap sideboard and worn
rug hit him like a blow in the face.

Miss Merrick was too thin by far, and there
were dark shadows under her eyes. Those hands,
that seemed to him as if they should always have
been laid upon the bow of her violin, were
stained here and there with ink, her pretty nails
short for the typewriter's sake.

" Have you quite dropped your music ? " he
asked abruptly.

She nodded.   " Yes, I could not keep it up."

" Please, Pamela," he said suddenly, and Jill looked up, quite puzzled, as her aunt went out of the room to get her violin, for the girl did not know she could play.

The colour came and went in Miss Merrick's cheeks. She breathed quickly as she laid her violin case on the table. Jill never forgot that little room, with the light of the fire competing with the candles on the uncleared tea-table, and Keith Middleton, the great painter, as human and jolly as any one else, leaning forward in their threadbare armchair, with his brown face all alight with eagerness.

With the light behind her stood Pamela Merrick. Her cheek was bent low over the instrument, and her sleeve fell back from the soft curve of the upraised arm and hand that held the bow. She was nervous, made two false starts, and then, with a bitter little sigh, she laid down her violin on the table and turned imploringly to her old friend.

" Please," he said, and this third time her nervousness went. Miss Merrick forgot everything but her notes. It seemed as if she was away in another world, able, through the music, to give expression to her own feelings.

Vivien, who had slipped down to curl up on the hearth with a rustle of bright flowered skirts, was the only person, perhaps, who quite understood. In her nervousness she pulled at Squibb's thick fur till he wriggled. Oh, it was almost more than she could bear.

The wailing of the violin suddenly seemed to her like the crying of a child who has always been cared for and loved, suddenly left sobbing alone in the dark. Then the girl drew a long breath of relief as the music changed. " It is getting all peaceful and joyful now," she thought, " the kind of music that makes you see pictures in your head. A garden, and the evening breeze whispering in the leaves. Two people in love are talking softly together, and watching the sunset fade."

When the music ceased there was a silence for a minute. Tears pricked behind Vivien's eyelids, and Mr. Middleton, seeing the effort it had cost her, could not ask Miss Merrick to play again.

" You have a great gift ! " he said softly as, panting a little, she sat down by the fire.

All too quickly the evening passed, and before it seemed as if Mr. Middleton had been with them for more than a few minutes the clock on the mantelpiece chimed ten, and he got up, exclaiming that it was time for him to go.

There was a hubbub of talking, laughing and shouting good-byes, but Miss Merrick had a word with her friend alone at last by the little white gate, careless of the soft damping rain that fell.

" So you'll show Vivien's picture of Jill to the art publisher you told me about ?  Oh, if only he gives her some book illustrating to do, the child will be in the seventh heaven of delight ! " Miss Merrick said as he slipped into the driver's seat of the car.

Turning to her with a reassuring smile, he patted the thin, oblong parcel in the deep pocket of the upholstery.  " Trust me, Pamela ! " he said.

" Vivien's whole heart is in her painting," she answered, " and the poor little soul has not got much these days."

" She has got you ! " Keith Middleton exclaimed with a warmth of feeling that brought a quick colour to her cheeks.  " And you can count on me to push your infant prodigy," he added lightly to hide his feelings.  " For your sake first, and then for the girl's own—poor kid ! "

He turned the thin silver key, and the car purred again like a sleepy cat.  Leaning out, he kissed her upturned face where the colour suddenly flashed up, then the purr of the engine changed to a roar and he was gone, his headlights making a blaze of light in the night.

With straining eyes Miss Merrick watched him cross the bridge, swing round the turn by the dead sloe tree, and a minute later the head-lamps dwindled to two specks of light like fire-flies, as the car raced up the steep moorland road, going towards London, travelling fast.

And Miss Merrick waited there by the gate, not feeling the cold wind, with her head in a whirl.

# CHAPTER X

## WHAT HAPPENED ON SUNDAY

" OH, Lambie darling, something utterly
hatefully rotten has happened!" wrote
Jill on Sunday morning as she sat curled up on
the window seat. Outside, the April wind sang
round the corners of the house and set the waves
tossing to the farthest horizon, but she was used
now to the rushing of the sea that was always
in her ears.

" Vivien and I have had a fearful row," Jill
scribbled on. " I don't know exactly how it
began, but I believe we just felt ratty. And she
said something I thought horribly cheeky, and
I flashed out, and she flamed up, and we went
at it hammer and tongs. Then I wouldn't make
it up on my own, and she wasn't going to,
either—so there we are, and things are as rotten
as can be here. What makes it worse is that I
scarcely see Auntie as she is shut up all day in
the study finishing a book that she and Vivien
think no end of. Brr! ping! goes the typewriter by the hour together, and she looks so

white and tired afterwards that I just can't barge
in and bother her with my troubles."

And then Miss Merrick called out that Jill
would be late for church, so the girl had to stuff
her half-written letter into her pocket, and rush
upstairs to put on her hat and coat.

On other Sundays Jill had enjoyed every
minute of that long, pleasant walk up the hill,
over the stile, and along the winding field-path,
while all the time the chimes called to them
joyfully. Then at last they would see the church,
with its great square tower that seemed too big
for it standing on the bleak hill top.

Now they were out in the lane again and join-
ing up with other little groups. There was Jim,
who grinned widely, feeling quite a man in a
stiff collar that rubbed his neck, and Thomas, the
carrier, hobbling along in his Sunday suit. He
winked mischievously at Jill, and as she coloured
and tossed her head quite crossly, Vivien giggled
in spite of herself.

Soon the chimes ceased, and the one big bell
above their heads seemed to say, " Come !
Come ! Come ! "

In this upland churchyard that was swept by
every wind that blew, there were no trees or
bushes, only just the long grass where primroses
and windflowers grew between the headstones.

Many graves had no names on them. " Where

strangers lie," thought Vivien. "Sailors whose ships have been wrecked here." And she remembered another graveyard, high on a hill top above a southern sea, where the scent of mimosa came in great wafts, and a flaming azalea dropped scarlet petals over the low stones.

"Perhaps I will never stand there again!" she said to herself. "Oh, poor old Daddy!" For the one stranger who slept there was dearest in all the world to Vivien.

As Jill took the heavy iron-bound door from her aunt's hands, and followed the others up the aisle, her eyes were held by the great east window in spite of her unhappiness. A marvel of glowing reds, soft blues, and magic greens, it shone out above the dark rood screen that had been carved in the days, when time was nothing, and craftsmen were proud to give their skill to the House of God.

Jill knelt down. "Oh, please God," she prayed, "help me to be friends with Vivien again."

A ray of sunshine glinted in and illumined her bent head. Then, remembering all the people who for hundreds and hundreds of years had brought their problems to this little ancient church, Jill drew a long breath and took heart.

Now the service was over, and with softly

shuffling feet the congregation moved down to the small side door, while the organ played gently in the dim church behind them.

Of course the day that had begun so badly went on worse. Lunch was a hateful meal. Miss Merrick made conversation with a rather ghastly cheerfulness, and Vivien, pointedly ignoring Jill, replied in the same vein.

When the meal was over, Vivien put on her mackintosh, for the bright morning had clouded over, and went off for a good tramp on her own, and Jill felt really thankful when the hall door banged behind her.

" I believe Vivien is jealous of my being here," thought Jill miserably as she leaned her hot forehead against the window pane and watched the thickening fog softly blurring the outline of the headland, while a grey, sullen-looking sea raced in over the wet sands.

Jill turned away and opened the door of the study : a business-like white-walled room, with an ink-stained cheap-looking desk piled up with papers, some chairs which did not match, and a square table on which stood the big, old-fashioned typewriter that never came out of its shiny black cover on Sundays.

Miss Merrick was sitting by a flicker of coals in the grate with a writing-pad on her knee. She looked up as the door opened and cried joyfully,

" I've just done ! The book is really and truly finished at last ! "

" You don't mean it ! " gasped Jill, astonished. It had been about so long, this book of Auntie's, that it had seemed as if it were going on for ever, somehow.

Miss Merrick said eagerly, " Oh darling, if only this book of mine is successful it may mean the end of all the hack work I've had to do. No more silly crooks and gunmen, but leisure to write what I want to write. And then we could all have a little jaunt to London. And buy some pretty things. You would like that, dear ? "

Jill nodded vehemently. She could not say how much she would loathe a shopping expedition if it would mean that Vivien, in her present mood, were coming too.

With a loving, motherly gesture Aunt Pamela sank back into the big chair, and drawing Jill on to her knee, big girl though she was, she told her all the plans she had made—thrilling plans that included an art training for Vivien, Beechdene for Jill, and a cruise for Auntie Pam herself. " So that I can see all the wonderful places Vivien has told me about while I'm still young enough to enjoy them."

" Hallo ! "

The door opened softly and Vivien's head

appeared. She took in the room swiftly. The two cuddled together in the big chair, and the sheets of manuscript scattered over the hearth as if they did not matter. And before Jill could jump up or Miss Merrick explain, she exclaimed, " Oh, sorry to butt in ! " and shut the door noisily.

Miss Merrick had been too absorbed in her book to see what was happening under her nose, so it hit her like a blow in the face when she went into the sitting-room presently and found Vivien, with her face white and set, sitting hunched over a book that she held upside down.

" What's the matter ? " Miss Merrick asked her rather stupidly, for of course she knew that jealousy was at the back of things.

" Nothing ! "

Pamela Merrick flinched. " What can I do ? " she thought as she went out and softly closed the door. " Vivien is my dearest chum in all the world, and she knows it, I think ; but Jill has her own very special place too. . . ."

Vivien, in quite a different way, was just as unhappy as Miss Merrick and Jill. Ever since the day, more than a year ago now, when she and her Pam had met so strangely, they had been more like older and younger sister than secretary and employer. Then Jill had come on the scene, and Vivien, who was jealous, like many affectionate people, had magnified many little chance remarks till they grew to seem like sharp thrusts at herself.

Though she would not admit it even in the depths of her heart, Vivien's quarrel with Jill had been because of this ; for the last two days, ever since it happened, the girl had shrunk into her shell, putting herself in the background when there was no need, concentrating on the hours of work in the study, and letting the old happy companionship with Pam, the rambles far afield with Squibb, and the firelight talks drop out with a vague excuse.

And now to come in unexpectedly and find Pam and Jill, quite happy, oblivious of her, talking plans, had seemed the last straw. The evening was a wretched one, and then, just as they were all lighting their bedroom candles from the big one on the sitting-room table the storm broke.

" While I think of it, Vivien," said Miss Merrick, smiling, " I would like you to get the last few pages of my book typed out as early as you can to-morrow morning. I'll be able to take a holiday once we get it safely posted off."

" I didn't know you had finished it, Pam darling ! " cried Vivien excitedly, good-tempered for the first time that day.

Jill, without thinking, put in tactlessly, " Yes,

*" I won't stand it !   I detest you both ! "*

Auntie told me before tea when we were talking in the study."

Vivien stiffened.  " Quite right," she said stonily.  " Of course, tell any one you like before you mention it to me.  Naturally your own niece comes first," she sneered. " But I was good enough to fill a gap before Jill came. Niece ! Niece ! I'm sick of the word. It's a shame to put me second now. And I won't stand it ! I detest you both ! "

Wrought up till she did not know what she said, Vivien glared round at them like a small trapped animal. Then she pushed roughly past Jill and made a stumbling rush up the stairs in the dark.

Unable to believe their ears, Miss Merrick and Jill waited tensely in the hall, and then, a second later, there came the sound of a key turning in the lock.

" My hat ! " gasped Jill. The guttering candle shook in her hand and her aunt snatched the candlestick from her and set it on the table.

" Take care ! You'll have us all on fire ! " cried Auntie Pam as she scrubbed the hot grease off the front of Jill's dress. Then she ran upstairs and tapped, and called, and tapped again on Vivien's door.

But though from inside Aunt Pamela could hear the sound of stifled, bitter sobbing, nothing would induce Vivien to unlock her door that night.

# CHAPTER XI

## OUT OF THE FRYING-PAN

MISERABLY every one in the little white house went to bed that night. Nobody slept. They all lay tossing on their pillows, turning the whole hateful business over in their minds and wondering what was going to happen next.

Just before dawn, in the coldest, darkest part of the night, the breeze veered, and Vivien, tossing out of a half-sleep, sat up in bed to hear the striking of the church clock on the hill.

Four o'clock !

" Why, it's morning already ! " she thought. " My last morning at Pam's ! By this evening I shall be settled in a back room in a boarding house with dirty lace curtains and a 'vacancy' card in the window. How vile it will be, looking for some sort of a job ! " Her lips twisted into a thin line of pain. " But I can't stay here after the things I said last night. I must have been mad ! "

Vivien, who rarely cried, fumbled under her pillow for a weary little ball of a handkerchief.

" And the book is finished now," she thought, " and Pam said she would take a rest. So I expect anyhow she would have told me she didn't need a secretary ! "

Vivien knew that was untrue even as she said it ; but something hard and bitter in her own heart, brooded over silently till it seemed twice as big, drove her on to hurt herself.

The first train for London left at a few minutes before eight, and there was not another for two hours, as Saint Pennah was only a wayside halt on a branch line. There was no need to hurry exactly, but she dared not go to sleep again for there were all those miles of lane to be tramped ; she could not take Eric, as she was running away.

Her head ached a little ; she felt heavy and dull. The hands of her little silver watch seemed to turn so slowly that once she doubted if they were moving at all.

" Time is a queer thing," she thought. " When we are happy and wish it would stand still, it goes like a flash ; but at times like this it jolly well crawls ! "

The first streaks of dawn showed in the sky at last ; the birds began to twitter in the hedges ; the sun rose over the tops of the hills, and it was morning.

Vivien slithered off her bed and tiptoed across the oilcloth. She pushed the window-sash

up softly and leaned her elbows on the sill. The
fresh breeze cooled her hot face.

In the eastern sky the sunrise spread out in
two golden wings; fields, hedges, the marsh,
were all bathed in a pinky glow. From the thorn
under her window a bird suddenly sang out very
loud and clear.

" ' Still in his wood the blackbird calls,' " she
whispered, choking on a sob as she turned away;
"'but there is one too few to hear!' Oh, Daddy!"

Then she bit her lip and pulled herself together.

Standing on a chair she dragged her battered
old suit-case from the top of the wardrobe, slung
it on to her bed, and propped the lid open with
the tooth-paste jar.

Memories came crowding back to her. That
back hinge had gone in Buda-Pesth, where
Daddy had been so ill. His old restlessness had
gripped him, and she had strained her case by
cramming in a pot of meat extract to coax him
with in the night train.

Those soiled labels, pasted so thickly over the
case brought back the past to her. Absently she
stared at them.

Berlin—Unter den Linden—with May sunshine
glinting through the boughs; Paris—narrow
streets of high, wicked-looking old houses, where
Daddy's friends grubbed along in improvised
studios. Their own tiny, over-furnished flatlet,

presided over by an enormous concierge with ancient felt slippers; Switzerland—Daddy had been better there; Venice—water lapping at the stern of a tied gondola and the pigeons wheeling in the square of Saint Mark.

She brought her thoughts back to the present with a jerk. Rooting among her things, she crammed a few necessities into the little case. A nightie, a sponge, another pair of shoes; Daddy's photo; the tiny Spanish scene he had left unfinished before he died. She felt she could not leave that to be sent on after her.

Vivien stole across to the wardrobe and opened it. Next, her little red dinner dress would go in. Precious little use there had been for such things at Pam's. Hopefully Vivien held it up, but it seemed absurdly young for her now, and she chucked it into a drawer disgustedly.

Sitting on her bed Vivien counted her store of money. There was enough for her railway fare to London and a little over.

Her savings-bank book went in next.

Then she dashed cold water in her face and bundled on her clothes with more haste than speed, for her hands felt suddenly nerveless.

A small white face, with great grey eyes that looked even bigger than they were because of the dark rings round them, stared back at her from the looking-glass as she ran a comb through her tousled hair and pulled on her beret. Then, fumbling in her coat pocket, she unearthed a pair of gloves.

Vivien knelt on her case at last. Now for it. She was ready, and it was still hardly more than daybreak.

Softly she turned the door handle, then paused and said to herself, " I can't go off like this, whatever has happened."

She turned back into the room. She ferreted for a sheet of paper and a pencil. Then, kneeling at the dressing-table, she wrote a few lines, while tears streamed down her cheeks.

That was all. There was nothing more to say except, " I'll write when I get an address." She wiped her eyes with the back of her hand and chewed the end of her pencil. Then she scribbled, " Good-bye, Pam. Always your loving Vivien." She folded the note and propped it up against her mirror.

With the greatest care she turned the door handle and crept out on to the narrow landing, carrying her case. There was not a murmur in the sleeping house, and the light coming in at the long window made everything look very grey.

She stole downstairs to the little hall where her pictures hung. Pam had been good to her, and in her heart Vivien knew she was doing a crazy thing. She stopped and listened. The silence was so complete that she could hear the thumping of her own heart. She drew a long breath of relief, for obviously no one had heard anything so far.

Only let her get the front door unlocked and she would feel quite safe. Very carefully she set to work. At last the key turned ; slowly, to prevent the creaking of the hinges, Vivien opened the door, picked up her case, slipped out, and closed it softly behind her.

The cobble-stones hurt her stockinged feet, but she dared not wait to put on her shoes till she was out of sight of the windows, for even though Miss Merrick and Jill slept overlooking the sea, Cook's room faced her way. The white blind was drawn down and she was a heavy sleeper, but one never knew.

Thankfully, a minute later, Vivien scrambled over the low wall into the lane. She hid behind the blackthorn bush to put on her shoes and then ran up the hill as if she had only a minute to live.

And the little white house on the sand dunes seemed to call to her, to draw her back, but jealousy drove her on along the road that led to the station, and to a step she would regret as long as she lived.

# CHAPTER XII

## JILL TO THE RESCUE

VIVIEN was very sure that she had slipped out of the house unheard, but for all the rest of her life she was to bless the fact that Jill, the one person whom she wished to avoid at the moment, was wakeful too, and heard the loose board at the head of the stairs creak softly.

Broad awake in an instant, Jill sat up in bed and listened. Then she jumped up, tiptoed across the room, laid her ear to the keyhole, and held her breath.

Click! It was the latch of the front door. Some one was going out! For a minute Jill listened in a silence so strained that she too heard the beating of her own heart. But there was no other noise. No barking from Squibb, who slept in the woodshed, so obviously the person down there was not a stranger.

Like a flash the truth came to Jill. " It must be Vivien ! " she said to herself. " Surely she would never be so mad as to run away like that ! But I can't go back to bed until I know."

Cautiously Jill opened her own door, listened

again, crossed the landing and pushed open Vivien's door, which was ajar.

One quick glance round the room was enough to make her very thankful she had been awake. The signs of Vivien's flight were plain before her : the tumbled bed ; the gap over the mantel-piece where the painting had hung ; the coat and beret gone off the hook behind the door ; and final proof, the suit-case was no longer on top of the wardrobe.

" So she has bolted ! " Jill stepped further into the room and caught sight of the letter. " How crazy !  Vivien will break her heart when she comes to her senses, and so will Auntie Pam !  And I can't open that letter as it's not addressed to me.  Once Auntie knows about this their friendship will never be the same. What shall I do for the best ? "

One thing to do suggested itself.  For a moment Jill slipped to her knees and hid her face in the tumbled blankets ; then, much calmer, she rose to her feet.

" I know ! " she said to herself.  " I'll track her down as quickly as I can and get her to come back with me before any one finds out ! "

Softly Jill crept back to her own room, and as she dressed she was thinking hard.

" Vivien will have to walk all the way to the station.  Luckily, it's only five now, so that gives me two hours to catch her up and bring her to her senses. But how unhappy she must have been ! "

Something of the feelings of a lonely girl, who could never really belong anywhere, and who had only one person left in the whole world to love, came to Jill's understanding, and her affectionate, forgiving nature wiped out the memory of Vivien's unkindness as a wet sponge will wipe a badly done sum off a slate.

" It is belonging that counts," thought Jill to herself as she slipped on her coat, " for if you are not born relations then everything is apt to come unstuck at a sudden knock ! "

Now Jill was ready. She picked up her shoes and crept downstairs. The front door, unfastened already, of course, presented no difficulties. Huddled close in the porch, Jill put on her shoes. Then, with her heart in her mouth, for she was directly under Cook's window, the girl stealthily made her way round the house to the back door. She intended to borrow Cook's bicycle without asking leave, and she hoped very much that its rightful owner had not put it in the woodshed, as she was supposed to do each evening.

Luck was with Jill, for Cook had come in late the evening before and she had left the machine just outside the back door with her mackintosh flung over the saddle.

" Difficulty number one safely over ! " thought Jill as she wheeled the bicycle down the path and opened the gate.

Now for it !

Once out of sight of the house Jill grasped the handle-bars.  Luckily she was tall for her age.  The machine was not much too big, she found, as she gave a little spring and settled herself into the saddle.  Pedalling wildly, Jill wondered how much start Vivien had got.

Now she was round the corner, and the first slopes of the hill rose up before her.  Taking a firmer grip of the handle-bars, bending forward, and panting a little, Jill struggled to ride up as far as she could, for every moment mattered.

" Perhaps Vivien won't listen, whatever I say !  But I'll have a jolly good try to make her see sense ! " thought Jill, pressing her feet down harder on the pedals as the ascent stiffened.

But her pace grew slower and slower as she wobbled to a standstill at last, and jumped off, quite out of breath.  " It's no use," she said to herself.  " I'll have to push my bike all the way up, and it is such an utterly unending hill."

Then as she toiled round the bend by the dead sloe tree, she bit back a cry of joy, for there, about fifty yards in front, was Vivien, carrying a case.

" There, I knew I was right," thought Jill.  " Here goes ! "

Suddenly the rise grew a little easier, and Jill mounted her machine again, and pedalled for all she was worth.

A minute more and she drew alongside.

Vivien's face was crimson as she swung round when Jill jumped off her bicycle and faced her. "You—Jill!" she cried angrily. "How did you get on my track?   Let me alone!"

For answer Jill pulled the machine across the path.

"Listen a minute, Vivien," she pleaded. "I just had to come whether you like it or not! I heard the front door shut just now, and I felt in my bones it was you—doing a mad thing. So I dressed and came along to get you to come back with me.   Oh, please, please do!"

"Shut up!" Vivien's thin face was white with temper.   Her eyes blazed.   "I shall go if I want to—so there!   Then worm your way in with Pam—I should!" she sneered.

Jill's eyes flashed. "You know that is rottenly unjust!" she cried. "And if you must leave, then say good-bye properly. Don't go slinking out of the house before any one is awake, as if you had run away with the spoons! And, of course, you are in the wrong, Vivien, and you know it, or you wouldn't act like this. Think how dreadfully Auntie will be hurt."

"Keep Pam out of this!" gasped Vivien.

" I can't ! Don't you see she is the one
who matters ? " remonstrated Jill more gently.
" You are her chum, and you run out of her
house after saying a lot of things you don't
mean ! Why, a kid of two would have more
sense ! "

Vivien turned scarlet to the tips of her ears.
" Mind your own business ! " she snapped, as
she tried to wrench the bicycle out of Jill's hands
and push her way past.

But Jill hung on, and, suddenly slackening
resistance, Vivien bent her head over the handle-
bars and broke into passionate weeping.

Jill felt more sorry for Vivien than she had
ever felt for any one in her whole life as she
crooked one arm across the heaving shoulders.
For a long minute the girls stayed still on the
white dusty road, while from the dead sloe tree
above their heads a blackbird poured forth his
morning song.

" Mop up with my hanky," said Jill at last,
" and come along home now ! Then no one will
ever know anything about this but our two
selves."

Vivien could not speak for a minute, but she
clutched the proffered handkerchief thankfully,
then, shyly laying her fingers on the handle-bars
to help turn the bicycle, she said brokenly, " Oh,
I'm an idiot, all right ! But I just felt I couldn't

face Pam after all the crazy things I said last
night."

" Cheer up ! " answered Jill comfortingly as
they came slowly down the lane together and
wheeled the bicycle up the path to the side door.
" It isn't the end of the earth just because you
lost your wool ! "

Vivien grabbed her hand and squeezed it hard.

One behind the other they tiptoed round the
corner to the front door, which Jill had pru-
dently left unlatched. For a long minute they
waited tensely in the hall. The tick-tock of the
grandfather clock seemed to echo in the quiet
house. It was still only half-past six. They were
quite safe ; even Cook would not be stirring for
another half-hour.

" Go up to your room," whispered Jill. " I'll
follow in a minute."

With her shoes dangling from their straps in
her hands Vivien stole up the stairs, and as Jill
crept out to the kitchen she heard the soft click
as her door closed.

Jill had never heard the French proverb, " To
understand all is to forgive all," but she felt its
truth just then. " How much nicer things are
going to be now that Vivien and I are special
friends," she thought as she lit the oil stove and
made some tea.

" Here we are, Vivien ! " she whispered, as she

pushed open the bedroom door with a brimming cup in either hand, " Drink this and you'll feel better, poor old thing ! "

But Vivien nearly upset the scalding tea all over the sheet as she impulsively stretched out her cold hand for Jill's warm one, and gripped it till she hurt.

" You're a brick—and I've been a rotter to you ! " she said.

" Stuff ! " muttered Jill to hide her feelings as, balancing a cup in one hand, she clambered on to the foot of the bed and pulled the quilt up round her. " We're seeing eye to eye now—so what does anything matter ! We'll have lots of fun together, you and I ! "

" Hear ! hear ! " said Vivien, and to seal their new friendship the girls joined little fingers and wished.

# CHAPTER XIII

## AUNT PAMELA GOES TO TOWN

THE next few days, with everything forgiven and forgotten, were very pleasant ones to look back upon. Vivien was a gay little sprite working at her beloved sketching with renewed enthusiasm, for Mr. Middleton, true to his promise, got her some illustrating to do, and she felt as if her career had already begun. The book for which she was to draw the pictures was a very simple collection of children's tales, but that did not matter. It was a start, and then came the fun of driving into Penzance to cash the cheque and spend the proceeds on a dainty silk scarf for Pam, a wrist-watch for Jill, and a pair of real silk stockings for herself. Vivien felt the richest girl in the world that afternoon when they drove back home after a festive tea, with the parcels safely stowed away on the back seat of the car.

It was fortunate that Miss Merrick's own novel was finished at last and posted off to her publisher in London. The release from typing gave Vivien time for this new, engrossing study. But life in the little white house was not all work and no play, by any means. Miss Merrick was so thankful to be free of the extra work she had struggled with so long, that she felt as if a load of care had rolled away, and the girls found that having her with them on their rambles was the one thing needed to complete the fun.

Then the clerk of the weather seemed to make up his mind to send along some spring at last. After a week-end of hot bright sunshine it seemed as if a softly green mantle were spread over the hedges, banks, and fields; even the distant hills did not seem so brown and bare. In the little copse up the valley that Aunt Pamela loved the primroses were fading, but windflowers nodded instead, their delicate blossoms filling the gap till the bluebells would come.

There was a perfect chorus of birds in the early mornings now. Jill was learning to tell them by their songs, as Auntie could, and high above the marsh rose the shrill glad carolling of the larks that made Vivien feel as if she must shout out loud for joy in the spring-time. Soon iris would lift their purple and gold banners along the banks of the stream, while the meadows would be sweet with the heady scent of cowslips.

" It's not in reason, though, that we've seen the last of the storms with April only half gone

over," said Cook pessimistically as she cut sand-
wiches for a picnic lunch. But Jill, who was
perched on the edge of the kitchen table, merely
grinned good-naturedly, and said, " Oh, don't
be a wet blanket, Cookie ! " But after all Cook
was right, as the girls and Miss Merrick found out
during a night that they were to remember as
long as they lived.

It all began with a red angry dawn sky that
told Vivien that there could be no picnicking that
day ; then, when she went down to breakfast,
she found Miss Merrick reading the letter that
was to prove a turning point in all their lives.

" I wonder what I had better do ! " she
murmured with a worried little line between her
eyebrows as she handed the typewritten sheet
to Vivien.

" Oh, Pam ! " Vivien jumped up from the
table to give her friend an impulsive hug. " How
splendid ! Fancy the very first publisher you've
sent your book to likes it so much he wants to
see you about it to-morrow morning at half-past
ten ! And there you sit and say, ' I wonder
what I ought to do ? ' "

" But what about you and Jill ? I don't like
leaving you for two nights, even though Cook
will be there, of course. Besides," added Aunt
Pamela as she glanced at the clock on the mantel-
piece, " it is a quarter to nine now, and the only

decent train to town leaves Saint Pennah at ten
o'clock.   I can't possibly get there in time ! "

"Oh yes, you can ! " said Vivien firmly.
" And you've jolly well got to ! It would be a
sin to waste this chance.   We'll help you to get
off, won't we, Jill ? "

" Rather ! " cried Jill, as she set to work to
gobble up her breakfast at lightning speed.
What good girls they were, thought Miss Merrick.
So willing to help her now that opportunity was
really knocking at her door.   And then, thinking
over this letter, and realizing that in an hour's
time she would be in the train, Auntie Pam felt
a little thrill of excitement.   Fancy, to be in
London again after all these weeks at the back
of beyond !   Her heart beat faster to think, not
only of the coming interview with the publisher,
but also of Keith.   She was sure to see him, and
perhaps they would do a show together.   Yes,
that short visit would be fun, as well as work, and
the girls would be all right, of course.

As soon as breakfast was over, the house was a
hurrying, scurrying bustle.   Jill dashed up to her
aunt's room and started to pack the things Miss
Merrick would need in the case Cook rummaged
out of the attic.   Vivien, thrilled to think that
Success with a capital S was really coming at
last, sprinted out to the woodshed to persuade
Eric to start in half the usual time.

It was a frantic rush. The hands of Vivien's small silver watch seemed to scamper round as she grew all hot and bothered, cranking furiously till at last satisfactory noises came from the engine.

" There is only an hour—no, not a whole hour now, only three-quarters—before the train goes ! " she panted, backing the car out into the lane.

Saint Pennah was a wayside halt on a small branch line, so there was only the one connection each day shunted on to the London Express at Bodmin. It would be a calamity if Miss Merrick lost that and had to travel up by the sleepy little local train that stopped at all the stations.

But many hands make light work. When Aunt Pamela, having given Cook some last instructions, came racing upstairs, she cried out in delight to find her packing done.

A very smart auntie she looked a few seconds later, with dainty high-heeled shoes on her pretty feet, and a silky grey dress, with a hat to match pulled down at just the right angle on her soft brown hair. One dab of powder and she was ready for the coat that Jill held out.

" Come on, Pam ! " Vivien shouted up the stairs. " The car is at the door and your suit-case tied on ! "

" Thank you, chauffeur ! " And, stopping

only to scribble the address of the boarding-house where she always stayed when in town, Miss Merrick raced down the stairs as if she were training for the hundred yards. One last kiss and she jumped into the waiting car, while Jill waved wildly from the steps.

Then Eric, honking loudly, rounded the corner by the bridge, and the little white house was left behind. Vivien drove fast, and the old car really seemed to know it was a special occasion, for it chugged up the long curly hill like a little Rolls Royce, and then, going all out, they rocked and roared and flew along the narrow dusty road to the station.

" I feel as if half the house was gone ! " thought Jill as she ran upstairs and saw through the open door her aunt's hair-brushes gone from the dressing-table. Then she scolded herself and said to herself, " You ijjut ! Auntie will only be away for two nights ! "

That was an odd sort of morning, the girls thought. Vivien came scooting back amazingly soon to say that Pam had jumped into the train just as it started to move, while Vivien hurled her case in after her.

Then they both mouched about the house a trifle aimlessly until cook rang the bell. Poor old Squibb could not make things out at all. He trailed about restlessly with his claws clattering on the oilcloth, as he looked everywhere for his mistress.

Lunch was a queer sort of meal. Vivien carved the cold mutton, or rather hacked away at it, with lots of energy and poor result, while Jill ladled out the potatoes and felt as if everything that had happened was a dream, and Auntie would come in any minute and explain why she was late.

When they had finished, Vivien suggested going down to the beach to pick up driftwood for the fires, and Jill, who was tired of messing about, fell in with her plan eagerly.

So they strolled out on to the lawn for a look at the sky. " Whew ! we are in for a whacking storm when the tide turns ! " said Vivien. " Put on your mac, old thing ! All those humps of cloud and streaks and feathery wisps up there mean a great wind, and rain too."

And then, with a sickening feeling of anxiety Vivien realized that there was a spring tide to drive on that gale when it broke, and that the two of them were left on their own—for dear, silly Cookie did not count—in a small, white house among the dunes at the very edge of the sea.

# CHAPTER XIV

## ON THEIR OWN

A FEW minutes later, talking and laughing, shouting good-bye to Cook, the girls banged the garden gate after them. The long grass pricked their bare legs as they hurried through the heavy loose sand of the dunes towards the grey, rather sullen-looking sea, where the white horses were beginning to toss their manes ominously under the lowering sky.

Now, at the girls' feet there stretched the curving line of seaweed, sticks, and broken things that showed the farthest sweep of the last tide.

" There was a ship aground last winter, and lots of candles were washed on shore," said Vivien. " The children came down from the village and gathered them up after school. It is queer, really, to think that we burn wreckwood in our fires. It's the salt in the wood, you know, that makes the funny bluish flame," she added, linking arms with Jill.

Now they were at the water's edge, and Vivien

stood still, watching the gulls as they floated up and down in the troughs of the rising waves.

"Oh, Jill," she cried, "wherever I may get to, even when I'm grown up, if I hear gulls crying I shall be able to shut my eyes and see this shore." She broke off and added briskly, "Let's make a start. The tide has turned already."

So they began to hunt about among the high reefs and boulders. Some were blue with mussel shells, others looked all brown and glistening with the long trailing seaweed that covered them.

Some of the jetsam was rammed quite hard into the clefts of the jagged rocks, and soon Jill's hands were soft with soaking and numb with cold. It was eerie, too, when she found herself at a little distance from Vivien, tugging furiously to lift a broken oar, while the slanting arrows of the first squall blurred the headland across the bay. Little beads of moisture collected on the brim of her sou'wester and trickled down her nose. A gust of icy wind ruffled Squibb's fur as he crouched in a humpty heap, for although he was supposed to be a pure-bred water spaniel, he had a great dislike to the weather whenever it did anything at all damp.

Jill pulled her coat-collar up round her neck ; abandoning the oar, she looked about for a cave to rush to. Then suddenly, through the driving rain a short stout figure in a print dress with a cap over one ear came flying towards her over the dunes.

" What's the matter, Cook ? " cried Vivien as she came out from behind a boulder with her arms full of wood. " Is any one hurt ? "

" It's me mother, miss," explained poor, agitated Cook as she got closer. " She has been took real bad ! And whatever shall I do, with the Missis away and all ? And me saying I wouldn't never leave you two young ladies."

" Never mind us ! " cried Vivien. " Of course you've jolly well got to go home at once. I'll drive you there with Eric," she added kindly as they started to run back to the house.

" There's no need for that," panted Cook as she clutched her cap, which a gust nearly snatched from her wispy brown hair. " Jim is waiting with the spring cart. ' Come back along of me, Auntie,' he said, but I answers him, ' No, not afore I've seen Miss Vivien ! ' And out I runs, down beach in my slippers and all," she added breathlessly, finding it harder with every step to get along in the damp sand.

Jill felt as if everything was happening at once. She brought up the rear, dragging the bundles of driftwood after her. At her heels came Squibb, creeping as if all his joints had gone limp, while his fluffy paws and trailing ears were all matted with sand.

*" What's the matter, Cook ? "*

At the garden gate Jill stopped and looked
back. " How big the waves are getting ! " she
thought, watching long tongues of foam dashing

(148)

9

up round the rocks, over-brimming the pools, and sweeping far across the flats where, only a second ago, there had been hard dry sand. A little prickle of excitement went up and down her spine, for the sky over the sea was one inky wall of rain, crossed and edged with fleecy cloudlets, while the squall that had gone over, a blurred mass, rolled up the valley.

The next few minutes were rushed and rather sad. Jim's white face, as he stood at the head of his big brown mare, made the girls feel awfully sorry for him, especially when poor Cook, all of a daze, as she expressed it, began to cry helplessly. Vivien ran to help her to stuff a few things into a cardboard box, while Jill went out to the kitchen and made some Bovril. " Cook had only a print dress on in all that rain, and Jim looks pinched with cold," she thought.

When Cook had gone, perched up beside her nephew on the high seat of the old-fashioned cart, the loneliness and eeriness of everything struck Jill almost like a blow, though she would not have owned it for the world.

" The wind sounds like a person lost on the moors, and wandering on, and crying," she thought as she paused and listened at the back door with Jim's empty cup in her hand.

Their own tea, when the girls got it at last, was a queer, muddled sort of meal. Vivien put the wrong cloth on crooked ; Jill, thinking more of the coming storm than of what she was doing, forgot the spoons, the jam, and the sugar.

It grew ominously dark before they had half finished. A sudden gust of rain drove against the pane with a sound like hail, while the tamarisk hedge, flattened one minute, tossed up like hay the next, creaked protestingly.

It was difficult to settle to books or needlework, and the vague, nameless dread that comes over some people in these storms was on them both. Jill lit the largest lamp, and they both sat very close to it. The wreckwood flickered and burned blue on the hearth, and the girls secretly felt ready to jump at their own shadows.

" It does seem queer without Pam," said Vivien suddenly, and then she went on in a low strained voice, " I don't know why I want to talk about things to-night, but I'd like you to know how I met her—and why she is all I've got."

Jill looked up, surprised, and the other girl went on tonelessly, " It all goes back to the days after Daddy died. Mr. Travers, the English clergyman in that little Spanish town, helped me with papers and all that. I did not know a creature there, for we had come from Buda-Pesth two days before. Oh, I mustn't think about

it. I can't—still!" She broke off with the
suspicion of a sob in her voice, then went on more
quietly. "Mrs. Travers was a stout, motherly
angel. She took me into her own house till it
was settled what was to be done. Daddy did not
understand business, and a man he had trusted
had let him down, so I hadn't anything left. I
felt I could have gone to that lawyer and killed
him!" said Vivien between her teeth. "But
Mr. Travers talked to me and helped me to feel
better about it. Though it was a wicked thing to
make a dupe of my Daddy, who was so clever and
brave and splendid, and who had as much money
sense as a child."

Jill shivered. It was the most dreadfully sad
story she had ever heard.

"What happened next, you poor thing?" she
asked gently.

"And so I hadn't a bean," continued Vivien;
"only fifty pounds from the sale of all we had.
Pictures, the curios Daddy had collected, my fur
coat—everything went. All but the two paintings you've seen in my room, and the little scene
Daddy had been working on that very afternoon.
Mr. Travers said I must bank every penny the
sale brought in, in case I was ever ill or anything,
later on. I was only just sixteen," she exclaimed
bitterly, "and I had not been trained for anything, and I could not afford to be trained

either ! The only things I know are the things that aren't any practical use. So when Mrs. Travers heard of a Mrs. Harris, with three children, who wanted a nursemaid, I took the job— jumping ! It was pretty awful. The weather seemed bitterly cold after the south, and the kiddies were so sick on the boat crossing to England, poor little beggars. Mrs. Harris liked ordering people about—every one loathed her— but I stuck it, spoiled kids and all, because I jolly well had to ! "

" How rotten ! " said Jill softly as she reached for Vivien's hand under the table and squeezed it hard.

" They went to Weymouth for sea air for the eldest brat, and a spoiled little fiend he was. We stayed in a boarding-house on the sea front, and I had a tiny top room I shared with the twins. I felt so self-conscious and hateful, pushing them out in a pram. A lady used to sit in the sun-parlour nearly every morning with a book," Vivien went on, " and she would jump up and give me a hand with the pram. Those were such steep, old-fashioned steps, and I hadn't the knack of managing. We started to chat, and on my afternoons off she took me out to tea.

" Auntie Pam ! " guessed Jill.

" Yes. In the end I came to her as secretary,

though I had never seen a typewriter—and could not spell. She has been marvellous to me, Jill, and taught me—oh—heaps of things I ought to have known when I was ten, and helped me to stand on my own feet again."

Vivien broke off, and a silence fell. It did not bear thinking of. Poor old Vivien, thought Jill. It was rotten, the things that happened to people. No wonder Auntie Pam and she were such chums. Jill realized she had felt jealous of their friendship sometimes, but envy seemed pretty small after the tale she had just heard.

Presently the girls spread the cloth and drew the table close up to the fire. This evening they forgave the big lamp for its smell of hot oil. The pool of light seemed like a living, friendly thing, keeping the darkness at bay. In the soft radiance the crusty brown loaf and glistening pat of butter looked twice as inviting as usual. Knives glittered and forks settled into place with a gentle clatter as Vivien laid the table. Then Jill, with a triumphant look on her face, brought in a huge frothy omelette on the largest blue dish.

"You're a marvellous cook, you know," cried Vivien as she drew her chair into the table. "Lambie must be a wonderful person if she taught you to make such delicious things!"

Bed, with a hot-water bottle, or even two, seemed a very pleasant place after a while.

Squibb, having deserted his rug on the hearth, and still missing Auntie Pam, was wandering from room to room with little wailing cries. Upstairs, the door of Cook's empty room seesawed to and fro, banging forlornly until Vivien went upstairs and shut it.

At last Jill closed the book she was pretending to read, and stretched herself like a sleepy cat. Vivien, lying full-length on the rug, looked up and yawned behind her hand. " It's hardly time yet," she said, glancing at the clock ; " but after all, it's horribly cold, and we don't seem able to settle to anything. . . ."

And then it was that they heard it, over and through the roar of the rising gale—a dull thud, three times repeated, coming from somewhere out at sea.

Vivien, white to the lips, jumped up and snatched the curtains aside.

" Listen ! " she cried. " Distress signals ! A ship is being driven on the rocks. We'll have to do something ! "

# CHAPTER XV

## A NIGHTMARE DRIVE

VIVIEN tore out to the hall and snatched her mackintosh from its peg. " Put on your oilers and rubber boots," she snapped, and Jill felt as if all her fingers were turned to thumbs as she tried to do as she was told.

Always, even after she was grown up, the rubbery smell of mackintosh brought back the memory of that little hall, with Vivien's face tense in the lamplight as she tugged on her boots, while out there the wind howled like a mad thing and the waves pounded a ship to death on the rocks.

Vivien, who had taken command because she was older, insisted on waiting till Jill had bundled all the woollies she possessed under her oilskins.

" We've a long cold job before us," she explained as she switched on her torch, " and we've jolly well got to see it through ! "

" What about Squibb ? " cried Jill, as the old spaniel came blundering round her legs.

" Open the kitchen door. I'm leaving him on

guard ! We may be out all night ! " answered
Vivien. " All ready ? Good. Now, one, two,
three ! "

Together they put their shoulders to the side
door and forced it open against the gale. The
wind drove in their faces, blinding them, taking
their breath. As Jill stumbled round the corner
of the house she staggered against the full force
of the gale, and her old school hat was snatched
from her cropped head to whirl away over the
tamarisks.

Vivien's hands were slippery with rain as she
wrenched open the fastening of the woodshed
door. The wind caught it and almost tore it
from its hinges. Jill clung to it with all her
strength as it yawed to and fro.

Vivien stumbled past her into the blessed
shelter of the shed. Her brain felt numb. She
wondered how they would ever manage that
nightmare drive that lay before them over the
crest of the moors to the coastguard station.

The car was cold, and consequently stubborn.
Icy gusts penetrated every crack of the ram-
shackle shed and whistled about their ears.
Vivien's face, in the flickering beam of the
electric torch, looked white and set as she fumbled
about on the dashboard, and forced the " twid-
dlers," as Jill called the metal antennae on the
steering-wheel over as far as they would go.

Then she stooped to swing the starting-handle in front.

" Click, clack ! Clickety, clack ! " Depressing noises were the only answer to all their efforts.

" This rotten car is as dead as mutton ! " cried Vivien.

And Jill's face was frantic as she gasped out, " Perhaps we shall never get started at all ! "

" No fear ! We're jolly well going to ! " replied Vivien. " Here, take hold of the starter and keep on with what you've seen me doing."

Then, as Jill stooped down Vivien slammed the bonnet up and fiddled expertly with the greasy mysteries inside.

" Ow ! " Jill gave a cry of pain as the cranking handle kicked like a horse, and the rattly noise inside the engine changed to a deep, purposeful roar.

Vivien was into the driver's seat in the same second, pressing her foot down upon the accelerator till the engine buzzed like a whole colony of hornets, so afraid was she that the car might stop again. But sturdy little Eric had no intention of stopping, and a moment later Vivien was able to reverse out of the shed. Jill took a running leap, and got on board just as they shot out of the shelter into the storm.

As she said afterwards, more by good luck than good management, Vivien slithered clear of the ditch. She tugged furiously at the wheel to get the bonnet of the car right into the teeth of the wind. Then, once, twice, and again, Vivien flashed her head-lamps out to sea in the direction of the sinking ship.

Anxiously the girls waited, and a moment later, through the driving rain and flying spray, they saw a tiny pin-point of light flash back an answer :

" S O S—S O S."

Vivien understood. Among the many scraps of knowledge picked up in her wandering life was an ability to read Morse. She jammed her foot down upon the accelerator and the car leaped forward. She could not bear to think of that awful sea, crashing full on a lee shore and the rocks of Deadman's Point.

She turned the car, and they crept slowly out of the shelter of the hedges towards the open marsh. Now the little rise of the bridge was before them, and a fiercer gust screeched in from the sea, and tore at the canvas hood. The girls felt, rather than saw, the thing snatched from above their heads and hurled to the side of the road. Somehow Vivien wrenched the car out of its skid, and back to the track again. But it had been a near thing, for the road rose sharply there, and on either side steep banks dropped down to the river that was racing in flood.

They felt the whole force of the wind now, and the thundering waves sounded horribly close. It was pitch dark, and in the glimmer of the headlamps Jill saw the driven foam lying like lumps of cotton-wool in the roadway.

Vivien's hair was flattened on her forehead with wet. Her hands, slippery with soaking and numb with cold, felt dead as they clung to the steering wheel.

Presently the road began to rise ever so little, but the worst was passed, and the thunder of the sea sounded behind them as they began to ascend the first slopes of the moors.

Vivien got in bottom gear with a scream of tortured metal as the hill grew steeper. On and on they chugged ; slower and slower grew their pace. A sickening fear took hold of Vivien. Then, as she expected, with a little choking gasp, the engine petered out, and they began to slither helplessly backwards.

The brakes screamed out as she jammed them on and heaved the steering-wheel hard over. With a scrunch of metal the car charged into the bank and came to rest with nothing worse than a buckled mudguard.

Jill fumbled wildly on the back seat and grabbed the starting-handle. Without waiting to be told she slipped over the side of the car and began to crank furiously.

Bravely the engine started up, but each time the worn tyres bit into the clinging, squelching mud they failed to hold, and with every attempt Eric seemed to slip more deeply in.

Vivien felt on the edge of tears as she shouted above the howling storm, " Give that up. It's hopeless. Find some heather, or anything like that, and spread it under the front wheels ! Oh, be quick ! The poor ship ! "

Jill obeyed for all she was worth, but the bracken had scarcely begun to sprout yet, and the tough, springy heather was almost impossible to tear up with wet cold hands. And then Jill had a brain-wave, and tore the car mat from the studs that held it down, and pressed it into the mud before the front wheels.

" Good for you ! That will give the tyres something to grip on ! " cried Vivien. " Now push with all your might from the back ! "

Jill gave a mighty shove, and this time, after a half-second of suspense, the engine took up the drive.

" I daren't stop to pick you up," yelled Vivien.

The wind snatched the words out of her mouth, but Jill understood. Staggering against the force of the wind, she pelted up the rough moorland road after the car.

When the crest was reached the track swerved away inland, and the gale, driving full off the sea, caught at the back part of the car ; all that was left of the hood suddenly billowed out like a sail !

Honking wildly, and quite unable to check their pace, Vivien and Eric disappeared into the night.

# CHAPTER XVI

### THE GIRLS SEE IT THROUGH

JILL gave a rather shaky little laugh as she switched on the torch. It was a ghastly predicament to be stranded on the "Haunted Moor" so late at night. The wind skirled about her head, and in the feeble glimmer of the torch, for the battery was running down, the ragged masses of the withered gorse seemed awesome and unreal—as if simply anything might be lurking behind them.

Jill called on all her courage and put her best foot forward. "Vivien can't go far at that pace," she thought, "so with any luck I'll catch her up before this rotten light flickers out altogether."

Her mackintosh seemed to be of no more use against the driving rain than a sheet of brown paper ; icy rivulets soaked down her collar, and up her sleeves.

"The wind feels as if it were a roaring giant that had hold of me, and were pushing me along," she thought as she plodded on. All round

stretched vast inky blackness. In the torchlight
Jill saw the slanting arrows of the rain glistening
like needles and spurting into the reedy pools
beside the road.

On she struggled, flashing her torch hopefully
every now and again till at last, when the path
curved away to the left round a great bank of
gorse, she saw an answering gleam of light.

" Coo-eee ! " The wind snatched the cry from
her lips, but the last dying glimmer of her battery
brought an answering flash, and she hurried
towards it.

" Jump in ! " shouted Vivien as Jill came near
at a stumbling run. " Every moment counts."

Panting till she could not speak, Jill scrambled
over the side of the car and flopped down in a
puddle on the back seat. Vivien skinned her
numbed fingers on the ratchet of the hand-brake
as she released it, and let in her clutch. The
engine gave a coughing rattle and they were
jolting forwards again.

Now, drawing long breaths of relief, the girls
realized that the worst was past. They were
over the crest of the moor, and the track, growing
wider and less stony, became almost a proper
road as it dipped down towards a cluster of
lights.

The next few minutes were rather a jumble to
Jill. Vivien jammed on her brake with a force

that flung Jill against the side of the car then slipped out of the driver's seat like an eel, and vanished into the dark to drum with wet stiff hands on the door of the coastguard's cottage.

Huddled forlornly in the driving rain, Jill watched sharp points of light flash up here and there ; heard shouts, quick words of command, and then the shuffling of feet in heavy boots.

" They've gone to launch the lifeboat ! "

Vivien had returned and was panting as she leaned over the side of the car. " It's as I thought," she added, as her breath came slowly back to her. " The ship is not wirelessing for some reason ; most likely their gear is out of action. And you can't see flares under Deadman's Point from here."

Slipping into the driver's seat as she spoke, Vivien swung the car round, and at a snail's pace they skidded down the stony track that wound almost precipitously into the narrow cove, where great rollers were sweeping in like furies over the jagged rocks and ledges.

It was too dark, in spite of the flares, for the girls to see the lifeboat glide slowly from the shed, gathering speed down the slipway until, at just the right moment, she took the water with a smother of foam.

Then, with the full force of the powerful engines, she drove through the welter of raging seas towards the doomed vessel, somewhere on the reefs off Deadman's Point.

The girls tried to raise a cheer, but the wind whipped it from their lips. Vivien's eyes were shining. " Oh, please God," she prayed, " let every one come safely through ! "

Presently there came the clip-clop of hooves on the rough road behind them, a jangle of chains, and shouts of " Whoa ! Gently, there ! Gently ! "

Jill, puzzled, turned round to see in the light of the car lamps great horses come trampling past, dragging the tackle for the breeches buoy.

" If the lifeboat can't make it, then they'll try and fire a rocket ! " Vivien bawled above the shrieking gale, and Jill shuddered.

It was a cold long wait there on the cliff top listening to the sea raging on the rocks below them, and knowing that somewhere out there in the dark a ship was grinding to pieces.

Jill felt the wind drive through her wet clothing to her very skin ; rain-drops stung her cheeks like hail, and great clots of foam came whirling up the path. Vivien stood by the bonnet of the car as if turned to stone, bracing herself against the force of the wind. Only her teeth, as they bit at her lower lip, betrayed the agony of suspense she was going through.

After a time more figures came trudging down

past them in the dark. These were women this time, wearing great wader boots, and their husband's old caps pulled down on heads bent low against the driving rain.

With never a look to right or left they struggled by, carrying their precious burden of hot coffee for the men waiting down in the cove by the slipway.

Hours passed ; they seemed like aeons ; like all their lives to Jill and Vivien. Everyday interests, Miss Merrick, the little white house, the things that had happened that morning, all dwindled till they seemed like small bright pictures of another existence. The only reality now was the tense, horrible waiting here in the dark and cold.

And then there was a stir and a movement among the people lower down on the steep. The girls saw a flashing of lights and heard a great shout. Mechanically, because the others did, Jill started to run, but Vivien yelled out to her above the screaming of the wind, " Stop ! we'll only be in the way ! "

It was all rather muddly, and dreadfully sad. Jill felt a choke in her throat as the bobbing lights grew nearer, and a little group of people came stumbling towards them with a weary, shuffling tread as if they were too dazed with fatigue to care where they put their feet.

Then the hangers-on fell back, and the girls, with a little exclamation of pity, saw among the sailors a man with fair rumpled hair and soaking tweeds, half carrying, half supporting a young girl who was obviously his daughter. She wore no hat, and her light bobbed hair hung all plastered with wet round her white drawn face. Water streamed from every fold of her thick navy coat, where a school badge glinted in the glimmer of some one's torch. She swayed dizzily as if she did not realize where she was.

"Poor old Lesley," said her father encouragingly, "put your best foot forward."

But the girl, as if she were only half awake, blinked drowsily at the blur of lights and never once looked across to Vivien and Jill, who stood beside their car, watching with wide pitiful eyes, feeling too shy to come forward.

"Eh! The poor little maidie! Who'll take the pretty love?" The kind women murmured as they came crowding round to stroke Lesley's salt-caked hair or chafe her unresponsive fingers.

It seemed the most natural thing in the world then for Vivien, with Jill shyly behind her, to step forward and ask that Lesley might come home with them.

"That's our car over there," Vivien pointed, the torchlight falling full on her white face.

*She swayed dizzily as if she did not realize where she was.*

" I promise, if you trust your daughter to us, we'll take tremendous care of her.  And we've got a spare room over at Miss Merrick's," she added.

The wives of the lifeboatmen saw the force of

that, for their tiny cramped cottages would be crammed to capacity with the rescued sailors. And so it was settled; the poor girl's father, too dazed with exhaustion to ask any questions about this chance that had opened out, half-carried Lesley to the car.

And in all the flurry and excitement no one remembered to mention that Miss Merrick was in town, that Cook had gone to nurse her mother, and that two girls, the elder scarcely more than a child herself, were quite on their own in a cottage built on the very edge of the dunes— while the worst gale for the last fifty years drove on a spring tide.

" I'll come over as soon as it is light to see how you are getting on, kiddiewinks ! " her father murmured, kissing her. But Lesley did not seem to hear, and she fell asleep even as Jill shyly tucked the rug up round her.

" Me and my missis will be proud to give 'ee a shake-down, sir," a tall stalwart coastguard touched the arm of Mr. Hughes, Lesley's father. " If ye don't mind it being all up and down like. But ours is no place for the young lady."

So, feeling almost at the end of his endurance, Lesley's father went off with his kindly host. To Dick Hughes it seemed like a fragment of another life, that morning, such a short time ago, really, when he and fifteen-year-old Lesley, his motherless only girl, had shipped as the sole passengers on the small tramp steamer, *Susan Ann*, on her return voyage to Bristol with a cargo of Norway pine.

Quickly the sailors who had been taken off the wrecked ship were shared out among the wives and families of the kind lifeboat men, the captain going to the coxswain and the crew fitting in as best they could. Every one had a hearty welcome, even the ship's cat, a black, frightened bundle, mewing pitifully as the shivering cabin boy cuddled it under his jacket.

The crowd melted away, and the girls were left alone by their car. Eric looked more of a tatterdemalion than ever, with the rear mudguard all buckled in, and only a ragged fragment remaining of the hood.

Vivien, who had been kept going by the excitement, like many highly strung people, realized how done up she was. Her head ached with the buffeting of the wind and she could have cried from the pain of her cold hands and feet.

Stifling a yawn she bent stiffly to the cranking handle. " Oh," she thought, " if only Jill could take a turn at the driving too. I feel awful ! How ever shall I get home ? "

But she got the engine going at last, and rather clumsily, with a scraping of gears, she swung the car round. Then, feeling suddenly that she was exhausted, dead beat, whacked, she pressed her foot down heavily upon the accelerator pedal and the car chugged slowly up the first slopes of the hill that rose before them.

# CHAPTER XVII

## DISASTER !

FAR from abating, the storm seemed to increase in violence every minute. Guided by the glimmer of the head-lamps, the battered little car ground slowly along.

It seemed to Jill as if all she had seen and felt to-night were printed on her brain for ever, and she resolved to take the lessons home to herself if ever she were lucky enough to get to Beechdene.

As she huddled shivering on the back seat Jill longed so much that it hurt, to have a hockey stick in her hands again, and to take part in the friendships, games, and fun of boarding-school.

Now the first slopes of the hill dipped down before them. Somewhere in the blackness below the swollen stream was roaring like a mad thing. On either side of the road, the high wet hedges, just beginning to bud, were creaking and groaning as the wind wore at them. Twigs and branches littered the lane ; eddying gusts caught at the car, and Vivien, tired out, was driving badly.

As they slithered round the turn by the dead

sloe tree, Jill's heart seemed to stand still, for the
car slanted perilously towards the left before
Vivien realized that they were in danger, and
righted the skid.

" I wish Lesley had stayed with her Daddy,"
thought Jill unhappily, then, pulling herself
together, she forced a shaky little laugh.

Now the car was bumping along the sandy
track that threaded its way among the dunes.
Alarmingly near, the maddened waves crashed
over and broke with a roar like thunder. In the
light of the head-lamps the frightened girls saw
long tongues of foam licking up to the very edge
of the road, and the spray was salt on their lips.

Once the bridge was safely crossed, the road
began to rise again, and the worst was passed,
for the hedges sheltered them a little. Volleys
of barking from the excited Squibb came to their
ears, and Jill cried thankfully, " Wake up.
Look ! Lesley ! There's the gate ! We're
home ! "

And then, when they thought they were quite
safe, the accident happened.

As Vivien braked sharply, the car seemed to
slither to the left in a helpless kind of way. With
all her might she wrenched the steering-wheel
round, but the worn tyres did not grip in the
squelching mud, and the car, completely out of
control, tore through the tamarisk hedge, grazed

against the stones of the wall, and came to rest, a hopeless, twisted wreck, on its side in the ditch beside the white gate.

Jill crawled out of the wreckage with nothing more serious than bruises, and a second later Vivien scrambled out of the ditch and wiped the mud off her face with her sleeve.

" Lesley ! " she shouted wildly as she peered about her in the dark and blinding rain, for the head-lamps had been put out by the smash. " Lesley ! Are you all right ? "

Only a low moan answered her, and Jill felt sick with fear as she staggered across to the side of the car and fumbled among the splintered wood and torn cushions of the back seat. A moment later she felt the torch and switched it on. Jill stood petrified, and a cry of horror broke from Vivien's lips, for there Lesley lay among the wreckage at the roadside. In the torchlight the girls saw the mark of an angry bruise on her cheek ; her hair was dabbled with the mud of the ditch, and one arm was bent under her in a dreadful, wrong sort of way.

As the light lit up her face she blinked quickly, and gasped out, " Hallo ! Are you—all right ? "

Jill dropped on her knees in the mud and said as cheerfully as she could, " Oh, we're fine ! And so will you be in half a jiffy ! "

Vivien leaned against the side of the car and

*There Lesley lay among the wreckage at the roadside.*

gritted her teeth as she fought with an overwhelming feeling of faintness.

"Luckily I did First Aid during my last term at school," said Jill, and all at once the mist seemed to clear from Vivien's brain. Up to now she had always seemed the capable one, but she was no use at all at jobs like this, and when Jill turned to her and said, " I want you to run indoors and bring me our walking-sticks and Auntie's umbrella ! " the older girl obeyed her thankfully.

" My arm . . . hurts . . . rather ! " gasped out Lesley suddenly, and there was a blur before Jill's eyes as she gently smoothed Lesley's hair and whispered to her encouragingly. Jill was sure that arm, doubled back so strangely, was more than sprained. But bandaging willing, giggling children in the gym. on wet half-holidays was a very different thing from this. Never, of course, had Jill dealt with a real broken bone, but when Vivien came back with Auntie Pam's umbrella, the yard broom-handle, and an armful of dusters, she just set her teeth. Remembering the instructions in the little blue book, Jill did her best with the hastily improvised splints.

Long afterwards, when she was quite grown up, Jill told some one that the nastiest minute in all her life was when she and Vivien knelt there in the mud beside Lesley, wiping the mud from her face, raising her head on a cushion, and coaxing her to make the effort and bear the pain of an attempt to make a move for the house that lay so tantalizingly near.

But the injured girl, badly shaken and in great pain, for the moment seemed to have got to the end of her endurance. Jill held the torch while Vivien dashed indoors and heated Bovril. But it was no use; Lesley's teeth were chattering so violently from cold and shock that she could not swallow.

Presently, feeling that it was now or never, Vivien and Jill half coaxed, half bullied Lesley to make the biggest effort of her life. Somehow, in the dark and driving rain, the girls helped her to her feet. Jill supported her on one side, Vivien on the other, as she staggered the few steps up the garden path and sank down on the chair Jill dragged out to the porch for her.

Vivien had lit the lamp on the hall chest. The soft radiance dimmed the light of the torch they had forgotten to put out, and the ticking of the grandfather clock seemed to race the beating of their own frightened hearts. But everything comes to an end at last, and after a wait that seemed ages long, though it was really only a few minutes, Jill persuaded Lesley to make another effort that landed her at last, in a dead faint, on Auntie Pam's bed.

Jill held the lamp while Vivien splashed water on Lesley's face, and then presently, when she roused a little, Jill very carefully slit up the sleeve of her coat and woolly jumper, and between them she and Vivien bundled her, half fainting again, into the nightgown Jill had put to warm by the kitchen range.

And still there was no time for Vivien and Jill to remember how their tired bodies ached, or how their wet clothes seemed to stick to their skins, for this nightmare of a night was not yet over, and there was another big job for them each to do.

# CHAPTER XVIII

## JILL TAKES COMMAND

" I'M going now for Dr. Grant ! " said Jill as she gave a final poke to the kitchen fire and scrambled to her feet. " You'll carry on here while I'm gone, won't you ? " she added.

" But the doctor lives three miles away across the moor, and the storm is worse than ever ! " expostulated Vivien as she set the smoking lamp down on the table and faced Jill. " Some one has got to go, of course, but not you ! "

" But you're utterly whacked. And you've done all the driving, while I lolled on the back seat. No, I'm sorry and all that, Vivien, but I'm taking on this job."

Vivien raised no more objections. In her heart of hearts she knew that Jill was right.

Resolutely Jill turned away, and going out to the hall, she picked up her soaking mackintosh from the corner where she had flung it in the flurry of getting Lesley upstairs.

Vivien put her hands up to her head. It ached violently. " I'm the older, and I ought to stop Jill," she thought, " but I can't, and it's splendid of her ! "

She went slowly across the kitchen and out to the larder, where she poured some milk into a saucepan and set it on to heat. " There's no time for a sit-down feed," thought Vivien, " but Jill will never get across the moor without something to warm her up ! "

Gratefully Jill drained the steaming cup Vivien brought out to the hall a minute later. " Thanks awfully !   I was starving, though I've only realized it now ! " cried Jill, putting the empty cup down on the hall chest, and flinging her arms round her chum's neck.

There was a lump in Vivien's throat as she hugged Jill. " Dear old thing ! " she stammered.

" Cheerio, Vivien !   I'll be back in two ticks with Dr. Grant in tow ! " cried Jill.   " Now, just you help me to get the door open ! "

Vivien followed her out to the porch.   Long trails of wet, they found, had driven on to the mat.   With a grinding sound the key turned, and the wind came shrieking in as the door opened. Jill, without another word, bent her head low against the blinding rain and disappeared, with a stumbling rush, into the night.

The wind was so strong that Jill found it almost impossible to get along.   Her rubber boots stuck in the squelching mud of the lane and felt as if they would be pulled off at each step, while the wind whipped her soaking skirt about her knees.

Where the hedges ceased, a fiercer gust than ever caught at her and flung her against the parapet of the bridge. As she clung to the stonework with her bruised hands, Jill knew that it was utterly impossible for her to make her way on the road over the crest of the moors.

And then the memory of Lesley's white frightened face came to her, and Jill thought to herself, " No one is beaten till they think they are. I must find some other way to get to Dr. Grant's."

The girls had rambled over most of the countryside, and Jill had a pretty good idea of the lie of the land by now. And she remembered that if she were to follow up the stream to the primrose copse, there was a little plank bridge. If she went that way, Jill thought, she might be able to keep in the folds of the less exposed parts of the moor, and work her way up to the doctor's house, taking much the same route as she had done with Vivien when they went to the cairn. What ages ago that happy time seemed !

Bent double, and keeping in the shelter of the parapet, Jill recrossed the bridge, then sat down and slid down the steep grassy bank. The water was very high, racing like a mill-stream, and when she flashed her torch on it she shuddered and switched off quickly, for the rushing torrent looked horribly cruel and evil.

Jill realized that she had done the right thing, even if the way up the valley was longer, for she had a little shelter, and it was possible to stand.

But it was a long slow business. Sometimes when the grassy bank sloped gently down to the water's edge she could make little stumbling rushes, but often Jill was forced to crawl on hands and knees over wet slippery stones. The roar of the waters deafened her, and she was soaked through, but she dared not leave the course of the stream, for the dark was strangely bewildering.

On and on Jill struggled till she felt as if she had been on this job for all her life, and then at last she heard the creaking of trees and branches, quite near her right. With a little gasp of thankfulness she crept through the well-known gap in the hedge and found herself standing in the little copse.

Jill flashed her torch round her. The wood looked an unfriendly, eerie place to-night, with the slanting arrows of the driving rain spurting into the stream and the wind thrashing the trees.

Jill put her hands up to her head. She felt

dizzy with battling against the gale, and her head
ached worse than ever. She flopped down on the
wet ground for a minute's rest and leaned back
against a tree trunk. Then she pulled herself
together. It took a huge effort to scramble to her
feet and stumble out of the sheltering trees on
to the windswept marsh again.

Jill knew she had only to skirt a turnip field
and follow the shelter of a high shale wall and
she would find the low plank bridge, over which
the moorland path led right past Dr. Grant's
house. It was only about another mile to his
door, she reckoned, and she had often been along
that track in daylight, so surely it ought to be
easy to keep to it even under these conditions.

Slowly Jill came down the steep slippery
bank, then she stopped and flashed her torch
out over the swirling expanse of dark water,
streaked with clots of foam.

A cry broke from her—for the bridge was
swept away !

For a minute Jill felt like flinging herself down
in the reeds and weeping her heart out, then she
set her teeth and took stock of things. The
brook was enormously swollen, and it looked
very deep—too deep, perhaps, to wade. All sorts
of things were coming swirling down it—tree
branches, a broken hurdle, a poor drowned hen.

Jill felt she simply could not face it. She

*The bridge was swept away !*

turned away, shuddering, and stuffed her fingers into her ears to shut out the awful roaring noise it made.

Then she called on all her courage and switched on her torch again. On the other side of the torrent the beginning of the moorland track seemed to beckon to her.

Without giving herself time to think Jill sat down and tugged off her boots, for they would only fill with water and drag her down. Then she pulled off her mackintosh, leaving her arms free. For an instant the wind seemed to die away, and seizing her opportunity Jill threw her boots across the water. " I'll want them when I get to the other side ! " she thought. She noticed carefully where they landed—one beside a jagged boulder—the other in the middle of a clump of low-growing gorse. Then she switched off her torch and stood with it in her hand as she thought what was best to do. If once the water got into that it would be done for, and yet, if she threw it across after her boots she would probably not be able to find either the torch or the footgear again.

" It's six of one and half a dozen of the other ! " Jill thought as she sent it over after her boots. " After all, I may be able to grope for it."

Then screwing up all her courage Jill waded into the water. It was bitterly cold, and her clothing seemed to weigh her down. The sharp stones on the bottom hurt her feet. Then she staggered as the full force of the current caught her, and the torrent swirled up to her waist.

Bracing herself against it with all her might Jill took another step forward. Her foot slipped on a hidden boulder. She lost her balance and pitched forward. The waters closed over her head, and she struck out blindly.

There came a roaring in her ears ; for a moment panic got hold of her, then Jill felt herself rise to the surface, and she took a big gulp of clean sweet air. Her frantic strokes made the water boil round her, but in spite of all her efforts— and Jill swam well—she felt herself being carried down stream. Her breath came in gasps now, and then, just as she knew she could not struggle any more, she felt heather roots in her hands. A second later and Jill had a firm grasp of the further bank, and very slowly, inch by inch, she could drag herself out of the clutch of the flood.

For quite a long time Jill lay choking for breath and shaking all over in the deep heather, then gradually her strength came back to her, and she began to crawl about to try and find the boots or the torch.

It was a heart-breaking search, and she was so cold that she would have wept, but she groped stolidly on, going over the same place time after time, though she did not know it, till at last her fingers closed on something round and hard.

Wonder of wonders, it was the torch !

Jill cried then from sheer thankfulness. It was such an immense relief to know that she would not have to struggle down that rough, winding track in the thick dark. The light was company, and very cheering. Her fingers shook as she switched it on.

With the torch it was an easy matter to retrieve her boots, and she sat down to put them on. It was surprisingly difficult to get them on over her ragged stockings and wet, bruised feet. But Jill managed it at last in spite of the pain, and then she set off at the best of her speed.

On and on she struggled, so worn out now that she could hardly keep on her feet. Her head ached violently and the cold seemed to have got into her very bones. Everything seemed a blur in her mind, except for the something that said to her, " Stick it ! You're nearly there ! "

# CHAPTER XIX

## WHEN THE TIDE WAS HIGHEST

FOR a minute or two Vivien waited on the step staring out at the dark into which Jill had disappeared. She clung to the door handle to steady herself, for her knees felt wobbly. Presently, after minutes that were ages long, Vivien saw the torch flash a friendly signal from the turn of the lane. What a pin-point the light seemed in all that blackness, thought Vivien as she snatched up the lamp from the hall chest. Quickly she turned the wick lower, for it flickered dangerously in the draught from the open door, then she held the light high and flashed it back for an answering signal.

Then, squaring her shoulders resolutely, she turned indoors, and the front door clicked to behind her. The slam of the door roused her and made her realize that everything that had happened was all true, and not a bad dream.

Mechanically Vivien dragged the rusty iron bolt that was hardly ever used, across the door for greater security. She crossed over to the middle of the hall and stood listening. The wind died down for a second and the tick-tock of the grandfather clock suddenly sounded horribly loud and sinister.

But she pulled herself together and went carefully round the house, with Squibb padding at her heels. With the utmost care she saw to every lock and bolt and window catch ; it seemed a marvel how anything could stand up to the pressure of that wind. The driving rain lashed the panes with renewed fury, and the thundering waves sounded as if they were coming into the garden. " And Jill is out in it—alone ! " Vivien thought with a shiver as she pressed her face to the glass. " Oh, if I'm ever half as good as she is, I'll do ! " And she went to her room to find some dry clothes and bundle them on.

The suspense and anxiety began to tell on her after a while. Vivien felt that if the waiting went on for much longer she would have to scream.

Wearily she crept across the landing and sat down by Lesley's bed, carefully screening the candle flame from the sick girl's eyes. Every detail of the wallpaper, of the carpet, seemed to cry aloud to her. " I won't count the silly old dips in the frieze ! " she resolved, but she did so, all the time. One, two, three, and the mantelpiece ; one, two, and the head of the bed. Why was not the thing in the middle? Her fingers itched to go and right it.

The girl shivered constantly. Abandoning her chair at last, she curled up on the hearth-rug. Squibb came and squeezed his warm furry self close against her. Every bone in her body ached, for she had been more shaken by the motor smash than she had realized at the time.

"Oh, if only Pam were here!" she thought. "Why had all this got to happen just while she is away?"

Then Lesley stirred, and with everything else forgotten, Vivien scrambled to her feet and bent over her. In bed Lesley Hughes looked a thin tired child, much younger than her fifteen years, with her short, still damp hair tossed on the pillow, and her wide open, frightened eyes.

Vivien pulled the bedclothes up more warmly, and whispered to her encouragingly, then she went downstairs and made some tea. The hot drink seemed to soothe Lesley after a time, and then Vivien and Squibb took up their old places on the hearth-rug.

It seemed a lot later.

Vivien stirred stiffly. "I must have been asleep," she murmured drowsily, "and I believe my watch has stopped." But then, as she sat up and rubbed her eyes, the grandfather clock in the hall chimed three silvery strokes and told her that her watch was quite right ; it was really only three o'clock, and the worse part of the night still stretched before her.

With a howling as if all the ghosts in all the Cornish legends had got loose at once, the gale redoubled its efforts ; then, as if a tap had been turned off, the downpour ceased. In the sudden stillness Vivien heard a swishing sound and a dull grating of wood against wood, coming from somewhere under her feet.

She raised her head and listened as if turned into stone. Squibb got up and padded to the stair-head, whimpering. Summoning all her courage, Vivien picked up the lamp and followed him. She leaned over the banisters and peered down into the dark hall.

A cry of horror broke from her lips, for the gleam of her lamp was reflected on a trickle of foamy water that oozed from under the sitting-room door.

" Whatever has happened ! " she gasped out. Vivien was a brave girl, and her father's daughter, but this unexpected peril in the dark seemed infinitely horrible, and she trembled all over as she went slowly downstairs with the lamp in her hand.

As she splashed through the water in the hall there came another crash of splintering glass. The swirling noise increased, and then Vivien heard once more the dull, scraping sound she had noticed before. It was the chairs, she guessed, skidding about in the deepening water, and rubbing against the legs of the table.

Panting a little, Vivien rushed into the study. She dragged the black furry mat from the hearth and pressed it against the crack of the sitting-room door. But as she stepped back, hoping that it was all right, a bigger wavelet swished a little higher about her ankles, and lapped into her shoes.

" The trickle in the hall is spreading worse than ever ! " she thought horrified. " And my lamp is reflected now ! "

Drawing back to the bottom step of the stairs Vivien watched this new disaster with wide, horrified eyes. She saw first a trickle oozing through the rug she had pressed to the crack of the door ; then a ripple, steadily deepening, widening in stealthy rushes over the carpet. Soon it steeped over the tops of her shoes, and drove her up to a higher step to watch it as it crept and spread.

Vivien's heart thumped till she felt as if it would choke her. Squibb huddled on the step beside her, pressing close against her legs in his fear.

Oh, why didn't the doctor come ? Jill, if she was all right, ought to have been back by this time. She looked at her watch. It was almost four in the morning, the darkest hour before the dawn, the time when fear stalks abroad and people's courage is at its lowest.

And then, when the girl felt at the end of her tether, she heard a scream of motor-car brakes above the noise of the wind and then a loud knocking at the door.

" That must be Jill come back with Dr. Grant ! " cried Vivien. " Oh, thank God ! " She felt suddenly weak with relief. Her fingers shook, and she had bolted the front door so securely that she could not get the fastenings undone.

Impatiently the door bell pealed through the house again. " I'm being as quick as I can ! " cried Vivien, not realizing that she spoke aloud. And there on the step, when at last she got the door open, stood Dr. Grant, with his weather-beaten face and kindly blue eyes.

" Oh, Doctor, where's Jill ? " she cried.

" Here I am ! " answered Jill, who had been standing behind him. And Vivien's arms went about her neck in a bear-like hug.

" Great Scott ! What's all this ! " exclaimed Dr. Grant, as he stood still in the middle of the hall and looked about him, appalled.

" A wave smashed the dining-room window." Vivien, a wee bit unnerved, rushed to him and clutched his arm. "Oh, are we going to be washed out to sea?" she cried.

The doctor laid a soothing hand on her shoulder, saying, "No fear! The high tide is past now, and the wind nothing like as fierce as it was, so don't worry! When I've seen the patient I'll board up that window for you! You've got a hammer and nails? Oh, good girl!"

Jill seemed too tired to take it all in. Lifting her feet delicately, like a cat, she paddled through the swamp in the hall and stood, shivering, on the first step of the stair.

Dr. Grant turned and looked at her. "Off with those wet things, young lady!" he exclaimed peremptorily. "Drink something hot, and tumble into bed! Sharp is the word!"

In a dazed kind of fashion Jill obeyed him and she stumbled into her own room as the doctor, carrying his case, pushed open the door of Auntie Pam's room, where Lesley was.

One look at the white face on the pillow, and the arm resting so helplessly outside on the quilt, told Dr. Grant all he wanted to know. He unstrapped his case.

For the next quarter of an hour Vivien wished she had three pairs of hands instead of one. She dashed upstairs and down again, fetching the things the doctor wanted, bringing an extra lamp into the sick-room, and somehow, in spite of her flurry, finding time to warm some milk, take it up to Jill, and stand by her to see the exhausted girl did not fall asleep while she drank it.

And now Lesley, her broken arm set and in proper splints, lay resting, for the medicine the doctor had given her had eased the pain almost at once. Vivien, with a little murmur of pity, laid her head on the pillow for a second, then, seeing the doctor beckoning to her from the door-way, she stole after him on tiptoe to the head of the stairs and burst out, "Oh, doctor! I promised to take such care of Lesley, and I've done this to her! It's all my fault! I was driving the car when it—turned over!"

And for the first time Vivien broke down and sobbed, with her face between her hands. Dr. Grant laid his arm comfortingly across her shoulder. "Cheer up!" he said. "That smash might have happened to any one! And you've turned up trumps, both of you! I'll go over as soon as it is light, and I'll tell her father all you two girls have done for her! By Jove, I will!"

Vivien, comforted, wiped her eyes and looked up at him. She had felt she could not face Mr. Hughes. But Dr. Grant's words seemed to put the whole thing in a new light.

"I'll be round about ten," he continued,

smiling, " and I'll bring the child's father with
me ! And I'll get the District Nurse to pop in—
unless her father wants to make other arrange-
ments for her. But you ought not to be left like
this. Jill told me as we were coming along that
Miss Merrick had gone to town to see a publisher,
so if you'll tell me where she is staying I'll put a
long-distance phone-call through from my house
as soon as it gets to a reasonable hour."

Vivien wrote the address of the boarding-
house out for him unwillingly. It seemed a shame
to drag Pam back, but in her heart of hearts
the girl knew Dr. Grant was right.

He took the sheet of paper, folded it carefully,
and put it in his waistcoat pocket. " Now I'll
just step in and have a look at Jill ! By Jove,
you've both of you done jolly well to-night. I'd
like to see Miss Merrick's face when she hears
what brave girls she's got ! " he added as he
turned on his heel and went into Jill's room.

" She'll be all right," Dr. Grant remarked to
Vivien as he came downstairs a minute or two
later. " She is fast asleep, which is better for her
than all the chemist's stuff in the world ! I say,
what a night it has been ! All because the worst
gale for the last umpteen years drove on a spring
tide. It may not happen again for a century,
so don't get the wind up ! Now just fetch me
that hammer and nails."

Presently, after a strenuous struggle with the damage done by that terrible wave, Dr. Grant and Vivien bustled about, laying an early breakfast for two on the kitchen table, for the dining-room was uninhabitable. The doctor felt as if he were a young man out in France again as he made coffee, while Vivien fried eggs and bacon, for they both found they were simply ravenous.

By the time a most exciting smell of fried bacon had filled the kitchen, and they were ready to sit down, the first streaks of dawn glimmered in the east. He extinguished the lamp as Vivien drew the curtains. The girl felt a lump come in her throat to see in the cold grey light a twisted mass of metal lying in the ditch beyond the broken tamarisk hedge.

All that was left of poor old Eric ! Oh dear, thought Vivien, what lots of jolly times they had had in that game old car.

Dr. Grant understood. " What rotten luck ! No use in dwelling on it, though ! " he said kindly. " Now, sit down and begin, or the coffee will be cold ! "

# CHAPTER XX

## A STRANGE LONG DAY

WHEN Jill awoke to feel Vivien shaking her shoulder it seemed as if only two minutes had passed since she had snuggled down into the blankets. "Oh, go away, torment!" she yawned. "Ow, I'm stiff!"

But Vivien took hold of her pillow, so she sat up to realize that the wind had died away and bright sunshine was streaming in at the window.

"Poor old Vivien!" Jill cried. "You do look like a boiled owl! Sit on my bed while I dress and tell me what the doctor said," she added, flinging back the bedclothes and jumping up.

"Lesley's arm is broken," answered Vivien as she scrambled on to the foot of Jill's bed and pulled the eiderdown up round her. "But it's not a compound fracture—the kind that is really serious. She will be able to use it as well as ever soon, thanks to you!" added Vivien with eager, shining eyes.

"Shut up about me!" There was a suspicious

quiver in Jill's voice as she sponged her face.
" Did he do anything to take away the pain ? "

Vivien nodded. " It was pretty rotten when
he set it," she answered, staring straight before
her as if she could still see Lesley's white scared
face. " But he gave her some medicine afterwards, and she dozed off almost at once. And he
promised me he'd go over to see her father and
tell him what's happened—so that we don't
have to . . ."

Vivien's voice died away drowsily.

It seemed like a dream to remember that
queer early breakfast, and then the first marvel-
ous stillness after the high tearing wind, the
shimmer of dawn above the hills, and the high
glad carolling of the birds.

Feeling somehow as if they were in church,
Dr. Grant and she had stood together watching
the clouds, shot through with pink and gold,
as they rolled back, and the glow lit up the sea.
The waves were as high as houses still, all white
and green and crested and heaving over, dashing
up round the base of the headland and swirling
far across the sands.

The swollen stream tore like a mill race between dunes all ploughed up and changed, while
the broken tamarisk hedge dragged its feathery
fronds in the mud.

" A wave smashed the dining-room window,"

went on Vivien, sitting up straighter and stifling
a yawn. " The place is in a fearful state ! Pam
will have a thousand fits when she sees it ! "

" Whew ! " exclaimed Jill as she pulled her
warmest jumper on over her head. " So that's
where all that mess in the hall came from !
What a gruesome night it's been ! " She shivered
as she remembered her own struggle to get to
Dr. Grant's. " It was too beastly for words
when I got out of our lane. There wasn't a hope
of being able to get along on the moor road, so
I worked my way up the valley to the bridge
by the copse where we used to get primroses.
But when I got there I found the river had
risen so awfully it had swept the bridge right
away ! "

Vivien stared at her. " I say, what did you
do ? " she gasped.

" I got across—somehow—but it took a bit of
doing," admitted Jill as she began to slam some
things into drawers, a process she called tidying
up. " But the water was horribly cold and the
current running like mad ! "

" You don't mean you had to swim ? "

" Yes," said Jill briefly. " And I felt about
whacked when I got to Dr. Grant's and threw
pebbles up at his window. He nearly had a fit
when he parted his bedroom curtains and saw
me," giggled Jill, suddenly seeing the funny

side. " Mrs. Grant put her dressing-gown on in two ticks. She lit the oil stove in the dining-room and took me in there. The light and warmth seemed just heavenly. I felt like a bull in a china shop, though, with water pouring out of my boots whenever I moved, and my skirt running rivers on her nice carpet ! But she only laughed and mopped it up with a cloth, while the kettle boiled to make me some cocoa, and the doctor stumped about overhead as he dressed."

But Vivien had never heard a word of all this ; snuggled down into the quilt, with her cheek resting on her hand, she had fallen fast asleep.

" Poor old thing, she has had a stiff time ! No wonder she is fagged out ! " thought Jill as she crept out of the room and downstairs to wrestle with the kitchen fire and try to get some breakfast for herself and Lesley.

House jobs, except for a few bits of cooking that Lambie had taught her, were not in Jill's line, and she felt as if the day was ages old before she had collected a tray to take up to Lesley, and fried some bacon for herself. Then, as it is always the way, just as the kettle began to boil the front-door bell rang, and she had to leave everything and go and answer it.

There stood Dr. Grant with Lesley's father, who looked very white and anxious. As soon as she saw him Jill turned scarlet. Of course, it was not any one's fault that the motor car had over-turned, but Mr. Hughes could not be expected to realize that, and he might blame poor old Vivien pretty badly.

And then, with a great feeling of relief, Jill realized that she need not have been the least bit worried, for Mr. Hughes hardly gave Dr. Grant time to say " How are you? " before he took her hand in his and wrung it till he hurt.

" There are some things one can't say thank you for," he blurted out, " and it's no use trying, but my girl and I will never be out of your debt —either of you ! "

So Dr. Grant had kept his promise to Vivien. Jill flashed him a shy smile of thanks. But before she could think of a thing to say, Mr. Hughes let go of her hand and almost ran upstairs after the doctor to the room where Lesley lay.

Jill rushed back to the kitchen, and there, with the door carefully shut behind her, she danced a little war dance on her own for sheer relief and thankfulness.

Dr. Grant was very pleased with Lesley this morning, and he soon bustled off, after telling Jill that he had spoken to Miss Merrick on the tele-phone, and that she was coming as soon as possible.

Mr. Hughes seemed in no hurry to go away. Now that Jill could see him properly in daylight, he turned out to be a jolly little man with twinkling blue eyes and very fair hair that grew low on his forehead, just like Lesley's. Jill soon felt as if they were old friends, and as Lesley had fallen asleep, and the doctor had said she must be kept quiet, he followed Jill out to the kitchen, perched himself on the edge of the table, and enjoyed the hot coffee she made him.

Lesley's father said he had already wired to his bank in town to send along some money, for he " hadn't a bean on him at the moment ! " as he expressed it. Also the old housekeeper who looked after his London flat had been communicated with, and would send him and Lesley some clothes. " And high time too," added Mr. Hughes, smiling, and Jill had to laugh because he looked so funny in a seaman's jersey that was three sizes too big for him and a pair of dungarees.

There was such a lot Jill wanted to hear, and she coaxed him to tell her how he and Lesley came to be on board a cargo boat.

" Lesley is crazy about the sea," explained Mr. Hughes, " and as soon as her school broke up—she's at Beechdene Hall, you know. . . ."

Beechdene ! Jill pricked up her ears. As soon as Lesley was better, Jill determined to hear all about it. But Mr. Hughes did not seem to notice her sudden interest, for he went on talk-

*Jill soon felt as if they were old friends.*

ing about the wreck, and dismissed Beechdene
as if it were no more thrilling and wonderful
than any other school any one might happen
to be at.

" So on the first day of the Easter holidays we slipped over to Bergen to look up an old college friend of mine and his Norwegian wife," he continued. " We had a wonderful time, and as if that wasn't enough for one holiday the kid must needs come badgering the life out of me to bring her back on a tramp steamer—instead of a proper boat, as I'd intended. So when old Captain Brenchly dropped in to see our friends one evening, the thing was as good as settled right away ! By Jove, that old tub bucked like a bronco ! " Mr. Hughes smiled reminiscently as he added, " I thought Lesley would have been fed up before we had left port two hours, but not a bit of it ! Well, it got pretty bad at last," admitted Lesley's father. " Everything on board that could come adrift got loose. Our cases were bashing from side to side, and the dishes in the cook's galley were battering themselves to pieces."

Jill understood. She did not press him to tell her any more as he turned and stared out of the window with eyes that saw nothing, and went on in a low strained voice, " We passengers were battened down and things did not look too good. The second anchor failed to hold. Then a tremendous sea smashed our wireless gear. Hours passed, and I know they seemed like years. Then, with a ghastly splintering sort of crash we struck the reef and heeled over. It was pitch dark, and there was a terrific sea running. The waves began breaking over the *Susan Ann* badly enough. She was wedged amidships. I for one thought our number was up. And so it would have been," he added simply, " but for two brave girls and a little car ! "

Jill felt thrilled to the marrow, for his praise, she knew, was Vivien's due. No one seemed to have found out anything about her own exploit in crossing the flooded river, and she devoutly hoped that no one but Vivien and Auntie Pam ever would.

And now Mr. Hughes was asking her about their side of it, and she soon found herself telling him all about her aunt and the publisher, and all the fun they had in spite of C.A.

" Aren't you at school ? " he asked, and Jill shook her head and began to talk rather fast about other things, for she did not wish to own up that she had failed in a scholarship to the very school Lesley was at.

When at last the door clicked to behind Mr. Hughes's retreating figure, Jill gathered up brooms and dusters and set to work. That morning seemed a confused, dreary round of toil, as if, like Tregeagle in the old legend, she were trying to empty a lake with a limpet shell.

Presently there came another ring at the front-door bell. Jill wiped her grimy hands on the front of cook's apron and opened the door to the District Nurse—a smiling, plump little person with steady grey eyes, a powdering of freckles on a turned-up nose, and wisps of brown hair straying from under her blue uniform cap.

"You poor thing!" she exclaimed; "are you trying to keep house all alone?" Nurse's voice was very pleasant, with a pretty accent that Jill recognized as Irish, as she continued, smiling, "See here, I've no one else to visit this morning, so when I've had a peep at the patient I'll pop into the kitchen and raise ye up some dinner! How's that for a good offer an' all?"

Jill's beaming face was answer enough, and Nurse's grin was a friendly one as she went upstairs to Lesley's room. Then her manner grew all professional and dignified, with just a hint of her merry smile peeping out at the corners of her mouth.

"How news spreads," she remarked as she unstrapped her case. "Fancy, half the country-side has come in charas and cars and donkey carts to line the cliffs and stare at the wreck of your poor ship. If those two could hear the half of what they're saying, it's proud girls they would be to-day."

Afterwards, with her tumbled bed nicely

made, Lesley lay resting, and Nurse ran downstairs to keep her promise to Jill.

Hearing voices, Vivien roused herself. Wondering sleepily why she felt so awfully stiff all over, she got off Jill's bed and discovered that it was almost one o'clock. Horrified, she washed and tidied herself at lightning speed, and ran downstairs, where she soon found herself perched on the edge of the kitchen table talking nineteen to the dozen.

That was a jolly lunch, and the girls felt as if they had known Nurse all their lives by the time the last mouthful of pudding was eaten, and Nurse jumped up, saying she must be off to the Upland Farm.

Vivien and Jill came out to the step to wave her good-bye, and with a businesslike ting of her bicycle bell she disappeared round the turn in the lane.

Shivering in the rising wind the girls turned back indoors. Vivien crept upstairs and reported that Lesley had eaten nearly all the dinner they had brought her, and that she felt heaps better. So Vivien and Jill, with Squibb in the middle, curled up on her hearth-rug and asked all about Beechdene.

Vivien thrilled to hear about the Guide company of which Lesley was so enthusiastic a member, while Jill could not learn enough about

the hockey teams—first, second, and third. Soon
Jill felt as if she had seen the rambling two-
storied building tucked into a cleft of the Dorset
Downs. It was sheltered to north and east by
the wonderful beechwoods, and open only to the
south where the land sloped down beyond the
playing-fields to the sea.

Little prickles of excitement ran up and down
Jill's back as Lesley talked about " Harrie "—
Miss Harrington, slender, incredibly young to
be a headmistress, without one grey hair, and
big hazel eyes that were a terror to evil-doers, but
that could look so wonderfully understanding
too.

And then they found that the time had flown,
and Jill went running down to clear away the
remains of lunch, but Vivien stayed on, for she
had an idea in her head.

The older girl began to tell Lesley all about
Jill and the scholarship she had failed for, and
how her mother had died, leaving her under the
care of an elderly lawyer, who had quite forgotten
what it felt like to be young. Vivien did not
feel as if she was breaking a confidence at all,
because she was so terribly anxious for her chum
to get to a good school, and not grow up with an
education of shreds and patches.

Lesley's eyes grew very bright, and presently
they began to talk in lower tones, so that Jill

should not hear. For the idea they had in their minds would certainly have to be kept a secret for the present from every one but Mr. Hughes and Auntie Pam. The question was simply this: Had Jill's share in the happenings of last night made her eligible for the Faith Anderson scholarship or not?

# CHAPTER XXI

## LAMBIE KEEPS HER PROMISE

TO Miss Merrick also so much had happened that she could not believe it was only yesterday she had leaned from the railway carriage window crying, " Bye-bye, darling ! Take care of yourself ! "

And Vivien, panting still from her sprint down the platform, had snatched off her scarlet beret and waved it vigorously.

Then the guard flourished his green flag ; the engine whistled shrilly as it rounded the bend, and the smallest, funniest station in the world, as Jill called Saint Pennah, was left behind.

A little smile hovered about Miss Merrick's lips as she settled herself in her corner seat, opened the morning paper, and tried to fix her mind on it. But it was no use ; the print danced before her excited eyes, only the presence of the stout, solemn old lady in the opposite seat stopped her from laughing out loud for joy. Suddenly Pamela Merrick longed, as she had not longed for years, to express on her beloved violin some of the joy that filled her heart.

It seemed like a release from prison to get away, if only for a few days, from the shabby house, the oil lamps, and the wind whistling drearily in the long grass of the dunes.

Her eyes sparkled as she fumbled in her handbag and took out the publisher's letter. Unfolding the closely typed sheets, she read them through again, dwelling on each word. Then staring straight before her, oblivious of the countryside that flashed past, she let her mind run riot.

Success ! Shy as she was, Miss Merrick did not want fame ; but money, ah, that was another thing. It seemed unbelievable to imagine an existence no longer hampered by can't afford—C.A., as the girls called it, turning stark necessity into a joke.

On and on the train rocked and roared, through Cornwall, over Devonshire, across Dorset, bringing her nearer with every turn of the wheels to London—and to Keith.

The sun dipped down, a ball of fire, into a bank of shimmering clouds. The light thickened; in front lay a pall of fog shrouding the great city, where here and there lights were beginning to gleam.

A smudge of soot came in at the open window and lighted on her glove. She flicked it off disgustedly. Suddenly Auntie Pam felt alone.

Turning her tired face to the glass, she stared out over the forest of chimney-pots. Her head ached.

Then as the train glided under the great roof of Paddington Station, and jerked to a stop, she let down the window and called to a porter.

Miss Merrick shrank from the crowd that jostled her at the barrier; the blast of hot air came up from the entrance to the underground like something tangible; her case seemed to grow heavier and heavier.

Presently as she walked along the grimy, less prosperous streets to the boarding-house whose address she had given to Vivien and Jill, she felt a lonely little dot among those hurrying, teeming crowds of people, each one intent on his own affairs.

The smell of cabbage, not-very-well-brushed carpets, and soot met her in the hall of her boarding-house. The proprietress, with her flat, plain face under her frizzled mountain of hennaed hair, said sulkily that they had a vacancy, and led the way up unending flights of stairs to quite the smallest, nastiest bedroom poor Aunt Pamela had ever seen.

A cup of tea restored her spirits, and then, taking her courage in both hands, she rang up Keith Middleton. " I'm in town quite unexpectedly—and I've taken you at your word ! "

she began a trifle tremulously, but his delight overwhelmed her.

The spell of London gripped her then, and the little white house suddenly seemed very small, far away, and dim.

Her friend took her out to dinner, and then on to see " When the Clock struck Twelve "—that glamorous modern revue she had longed to see. To Pamela Merrick it seemed as if the years had rolled back to sense again the hush of expectancy in the dim, crowded theatre, to taste the sweetness of the chocolates Keith brought for her and to smell the fragrance of his cigarette.

When they came out of the theatre the rain was lashing the pavements, but Mr. Middleton was there to drive her back in his beautiful car.

As she peeped out at the wet streets through a windscreen all diamonded with rain, Miss Merrick's thoughts flew to her two girls and fat, furry old Squibb. Every one in the house on the sand dunes would be in bed and asleep now, dreaming perhaps of the wider life her success might open out for them.

Aunt Pamela could not sleep that night. Her slit of a room was high up under the roof, and the bed was very hard. Now and then a fiercer gust of wind screeched among the chimney stacks. Somehow she could not get the thought of the girls out of her head. And when at last

Miss Merrick closed her eyes towards morning, she started up, broad awake again, to fancy that she heard Jill's frightened voice calling to her wildly.

Further sleep was impossible, and, oppressed by a dead weight of anxiety, Miss Merrick punched up her pillow and lay, pretending to read, while the street lamps grew pale in the dawn and the first gleam of sun glistened on the wet roofs.

The boarding-house was not a very nice one. The guests sat at a long table; her breakfast egg tasted of straw, and the old gentleman at her side slopped his coffee all over his saucer.

Slowly the hands of the black marble clock on the mantelpiece moved round. Soon it would be time to catch her bus for Fleet Street. Oh, Aunt Pamela thought suddenly, if only the girls were with her, to laugh at the petty discomforts and to share in the thrill. So much hung on that momentous interview, and she had to face it alone.

" Brr ! Ping ! "

" Yer wanted on the phone." The pasty-faced little maid, with her cap slanted over one ear, put her agitated head round the door, " 'Ere, Miss Merrick ! Quick ! " she panted.

Aunt Pamela ran.

Dr. Grant's gruff voice, speaking from all those miles away, set her heart jumping. " Of course

I'm coming ! " she cried, too anxious to think of the details of her journey. Then Miss Merrick broke off, for he was speaking again—shouting something about an accident—and some one— for the life of her she couldn't catch who it was— badly hurt.

" What do you say ? Who is it ? How did it happen ? " she was beginning in an agony of apprehension, but the telephone operator, with a crisp, " Three minutes, please ! " cut them off.

There was only one thought in Miss Merrick's bewildered mind, and that was that Keith would help her. Her fingers shook as she dialled his modern, expensive flat. Luckily he was at home, and the urgency in her trembling tones brought him driving through the traffic at the pace of a fire-engine.

By the time his authoritative pull at the bell had brought the little maid scurrying out of the coal hole like a hare, Aunt Pamela had collected her wits, paid her bill, and stuffed her evening dress into her case with shaking hands.

One idea was firmly fixed in her mind—she must get hold of Lambie. And Miss Merrick never gave another thought to the waiting publisher as she ran down the stairs to where Mr. Middleton waited on the steps.

" Oh, bless you for coming ! " she cried when she saw the car.

Keith Middleton wasted no time in useless questioning. He let in his clutch and they shot away through the maze of mean streets. Incredibly soon he drew up outside the little house where Lambie had gone to live with her brother. Miss Merrick jumped out and ran up the steps. As the door closed behind her Mr. Middleton turned his car and was off like a flash for the expensive shops.

Amazingly soon he returned with the back of the car piled high with the things he had bought —Bovril and jellies in delicious profusion, and a huge basket of fruit—golden oranges, rosy-cheeked apples, and blue, luscious grapes in their soft cotton wool.

He had not long to wait. Poor Lambie, struck all of a daze, as she expressed it, could only say over and over again, " I promised my darling I would come if ever she wanted me ! " as she came hurrying down the steps carrying a bulging raffia bag.

Her brother, of course, was out at work, so Miss Merrick had scribbled a little note for him, to explain what had happened, and the next-door neighbour, who had seen the car drive up, popped her head over the fence to see what the matter was, and promised willingly to pack and send Lambie's trunk on after her.

Miss Merrick locked the door, for Lambie's

hands were shaking, and she gave the key to the friendly neighbour and ran down the steps.

" Oh, Keith ! " was all she could say when she saw the boxes in the car. But he would not let her thank him, only settled Lambie comfortably on the back seat and tucked the rug up round her.

Miss Merrick jumped up in front beside him. He turned the thin key on the dashboard ; the engine purred, then roared, and they were off.

Aunt Pamela's hands were clenched on her knees in a fever of impatience, for the pace seemed unbearably slow as Mr. Middleton guided the powerful car through the narrow, twisting streets with their thronging traffic.

Presently the wide, concrete sweep of the Great West Road stretched before them ; down went Keith Middleton's foot on the accelerator pedal, and the car leaped forward like a greyhound freed from the slips.

The suburbs were left behind them now. It did not seem very long before they were speeding across the swelling Wiltshire downs and through white-walled Dorset villages, and at last rushing down red Devon combes. At last came a halt at a lonely grey inn on the windswept Cornish moors, and they enjoyed a hurried cup of tea. Then on again in the gathering dusk up the steep hill into Saint Pennah, where the lights behind

the drawn blinds glowed like patches of amber,
and the signboard of the Blue Boar Inn creaked
and swung in the freshening breeze. They
skirted the pond under the churchyard wall and
then took the lane that wound across the upland
fields.

The salt breeze was cool on their tired faces
now, and as the car rushed along they heard
the thundering roar of an angry sea breaking
on the rocks and hard sands.

Now the first slopes of the hill yawned before
them; from somewhere below came the sound of
the swollen stream, and the wind soughed in the
dead sloe tree.

But they had no eyes for anything else, for
there, across the bay, one little patch of light in
all the darkening grey, gleamed the lamp in the
window of the house among the dunes.

# CHAPTER XXII

## THE ENDING OF THE STRANGE LONG DAY

TO the frightened girls in the little white house on the sands twilight seemed to fall earlier than usual that evening. Before they had half finished tea the corners of the kitchen were growing very dim and dusky, and they had to light the lamp.

Wearily Jill pushed her plate away and went and ferreted on the study book-shelves for a railway time-table. Vivien came and peeped over her shoulder, saying, " Let me help you. Time-tables eat out of my hand ! "

But con the Bradshaw as they might, there was no getting over the fact that the last train from London had reached Saint Pennah more than an hour ago, and if Miss Merrick did not come in a very few minutes, then they must give her up and face another night on their own.

It was very cold for late April. Vivien shivered as she crossed the hall and opened the front door. With hands thrust deeply into the pockets of her old blue cardigan, she stood on the step, telling herself that a thousand things might have delayed Pam and that perhaps she was coming after all.

Then, marvellously, as her last hope was fading, she saw the lights of a car come racing down the steep moorland road. A startled exclamation broke from her; she saw the withered branches of the dead sloe tree thrown into sharp relief as the driver rounded the bend. Holding her breath Vivien stared as if she could not believe her eyes. The hills were dark again now, and the dazzling beam of light was nearer, speeding towards her over the marsh.

She turned and tore indoors.

" Jill ! " she shrilled from the foot of the stairs. " Come and look ! Quick ! "

With a blare on the horn and a quick dimming of the lamps the car rounded the bend of the lane and slackened speed. " It's Mr. Middleton —with Pam ! And some one else ! " cried Vivien, and her excited shout brought Jill flying out of the house as fast as she could set foot to the ground. The garden gate crashed behind her as she sprinted out into the road, with Squibb at her heels barking loudly.

Almost before the car had glided to a stop the girls, laughing, crying, and exclaiming all at once, were up on the running-board.

" My promises aren't pie-crust, ducky ! I

said I'd come if ever you wanted me," Mrs. Lambert whispered in Jill's ear as she hugged her tightly. Vivien snuggled her head down on her friend's shoulder and said rapturously, " Everything will be all right, now you've come."

Miss Merrick held her closer, and then, looking up, exclaimed, " What's that car in the ditch ? Have you had a motor smash ? Who is hurt ? " Her voice rose, sharp with fear, but neither of the girls could answer.

For a second, with wide, horrified eyes, Miss Merrick stared at the heap of twisted wreckage by the gate ; then she turned and rushed indoors, followed by Mr. Middleton.

Vivien sprang forward and clutched her arm, and poured out a breathless, disjointed account of the previous night into her ears. It did not bear thinking of, and Miss Merrick could only gasp out, " Thank God you're all safe ! "

Keith Middleton's soothing hand on her shoulder calmed her nerves, but it was with a very anxious heart that she turned away and ran up to the room where Lesley was.

She tapped softly on the door, and hearing a shy voice call " Come in ! " she opened it.

The girl was lying propped high on a miscellaneous collection of pillows, trying to do a crossword puzzle with her left hand, while her broken arm, all in splints, lay outside on the coverlet.

She left off chewing her pencil and looked up, expecting to see Jill or Vivien.  Lesley Hughes always remembered her first sight of Jill's pretty aunt as she came up to the bedside and asked her how she was getting on.

The girl stammered out a shy reply, and Miss Merrick bent over and kissed her before she sat down and talked to Lesley in such a friendly, jolly way that she quite forgot to be shy of this well-known author, and chatted away to Miss Merrick as if she had known her all her life.

Downstairs there was a hubbub as Vivien, Jill, and Lambie unpacked the car of all the good things that had been so carefully stowed away in it that morning, and Jill cried excitedly, " The hall chest looks like the counter of a shop ! "

Presently Miss Merrick, white and tired-looking, came slowly down the stairs.  Lambie set down the box she was bringing in and went over to her, saying, " Just tell me where everything is kept, and I'll get some supper on the table. You're wanting it, I know."

Her sympathy was wonderfully comforting, and Auntie Pam's eyes filled as she gave Mrs. Lambert's arm a little squeeze and led the way to the kitchen.

As she opened the door Lambie held up her hands in pretended horror at the confusion within.  " What a pickle the young ladies have got into ! " she cried as she looked about her. " I didn't think it could be done in just two days. I didn't indeed ! "

And then, remembering their struggles, Jill and Vivien, who had followed her in, burst out laughing too.

" Shoo ! " cried Mrs. Lambert. " Leave this to me, duckies ! " Wasting no more time, Lambie took the pins out of her hat, tied an apron round her waist, and set to work.

The fire soon woke into life at Lambie's magic, as Jill called it ; but Mrs. Lambert, on her knees on the rag rug, looked up and smiled when Jill put her head round the door.

" It isn't magic, it's an old newspaper, ducky, and raking out all them ashes underneath ! You never thought of that, I'll be bound."

Mr. Middleton found a torch and went off by himself to unlock the sitting-room door. He soon came back, and he strode rapidly up and down the kitchen, talking learnedly to Auntie Pam, who was trying to help Lambie, all about insurance, and the damages that were due.

Vivien lit the big lamp and laid the cloth, while Jill took the plates down from the dresser and fetched a crusty brown loaf.

Often Jill paused to look fondly across at Lambie where she stood before the range. A brooch at the neck of Lambie's voluminous black dress caught the firelight, and the rustle of her apron as she moved to and fro between the table and the stove were as music in Jill's ears.

They had only just finished supper when the front-door bell rang, and wondering who on earth it could be so late, Lambie bustled out to the porch. Dr. Grant stood on the step, and his face lit up as soon as he saw her there. " What a mercy you've come ! " he cried. Then seeing Aunt Pamela just behind Lambie he hastened forward and gripped her out-stretched fingers hard.

" I've never been so thankful to see any one in all my life ! " he cried, and then added, with apparent irrelevance, " Have you had an evening paper ? "

Aunt Pamela stared at him, feeling quite puzzled, but the doctor's blue eyes twinkled merrily. " I was through Saint Pennah this evening," he explained, " and I saw a poster up outside the station that sent me hurrying in to buy a copy ! " Smiling, he unfolded the paper and pointed to a paragraph he had marked.

The headlines danced before Miss Merrick's astonished eyes. Completely bewildered, she put on her horn-rimmed spectacles and read aloud :

" Heroic girls drive car to rescue of doomed ship. Distress signals seen from windows of lonely house. . . ." Her voice faltered. There was a choke in her throat. It was impossible for her to go on reading.

This was Mr. Middleton's opportunity.

" Let me, Pamela ! " he said, gently taking the paper out of her trembling hands. Then amid a breathless stillness he read aloud the account of the wreck of the cargo boat *Susan Ann*, and how two brave girls had warned the coastguard and saved the lives of all on board.

Jill turned scarlet. Vivien twisted her hands together in an agony of shyness, but Dr. Grant surprised every one by exclaiming, " And that's not the half of it ! "

He unstrapped his case and got out a sodden, crushed-looking mackintosh, which he waved before their bewildered eyes.

" I could not make out how Jill got to my house," he said. " For no human being could have stood upright on the moor in the teeth of the gale that was blowing when she came to me. So I put on my considering cap and did a spot of Sherlock Holmes on my own, and realized that she must have taken another way. So this afternoon I went up to the copse where the plank bridge had been, and, as I expected, I found this mackintosh."

There was not a vestige of colour in Aunt Pamela's cheeks ; Vivien, her face aglow, crept nearer and slipped an arm round her waist. Jill felt she did not know where to hide her head. If it had not been for Mr. Middleton's kindly hand on her shoulder she would have turned and bolted upstairs in the dark.

There was a breathless silence as the doctor continued, " What can we say to the quiet, considered courage of a girl who will swim a flooded torrent in pitch darkness and bitter cold, when she is dead beat, and then comes quietly home and says nothing about it ? "

" For she's a jolly good fellow ! " Keith Middleton's deep voice began to hum softly, and the chorus swelled out quite loudly as every one joined in with a will, " And so say all of us ! "

But Lambie had her apron to her eyes, crying for joy and pride in the girl she loved so much.

# CHAPTER XXIII

## THINGS BEGIN TO MOVE

BEFORE the hubbub had died down the bell rang again, and Lambie opened the door to Lesley's father. His housekeeper had wasted no time, Mr. Hughes explained, for as soon as she had got his wire she had packed a suit-case, taken a taxi to Paddington station as quickly as she could, and caught the next train. Mr. Hughes had parked her at the Upland Farm, as he expressed it, and taken a room at the Blue Boar Inn for himself, since he could not trespass any longer on the kindness of the coast-guard's wife, who had a sick baby.

Mr. Hughes' intention was to travel back to town with Lesley to-morrow, but when she heard this Miss Merrick put her foot down. Dr. Grant backed her up, so it was finally settled that the girl should stay where she was for a week at least, to get completely over the shock.

After that, of course, she would come to no harm, and, with her arm in splints and properly strapped, she might even return to school in due course, though naturally there would be no swimming or games for a long while.

And then, Jill wondered why, since everything was so satisfactorily settled, her aunt, with Mr. Middleton and Mr. Hughes, went up to Lesley's room and stayed there talking for so very long.

Dr. Grant, who had another case to see, went off pretty soon, and as soon as the door closed behind him Vivien slipped away and joined the confabulation upstairs. Jill felt quite puzzled to know what they were all discussing so animatedly up there, but Lambie, who had had a word with Lesley's father, kept asking the girl's help with one job after another, and Jill could not find a minute to go and join them.

Vivien's eyes were starry when at last she came down with Auntie Pam, who had a pink, excited colour in her cheeks. Then the two men got into the car and drove away ; Mr. Middleton said he also was staying at the " Blue Boar " for the present.

Next there was a flurry of making up beds and airing blankets, and it was quite late when goodnights were said.

The next few days seemed like a dream to Jill. At long last Thomas the carrier brought Lambie's trunk, and when she had unpacked and settled into Cook's old room, Jill felt as if she had come

to live with them for always, and would not
suddenly be spirited away.

Things would perhaps have fallen flat after
Lesley and her father went back to town and
all the excitement was over, if it had not been
for Keith Middleton, who was still at the Blue
Boar Inn at St. Pennah.  And if Miss Merrick
sometimes wondered about the commissions he
must be losing and what his London friends
would be making of his long absence, she said
nothing about it and was content to enjoy each
moment as it passed and be with her old friend
all she could.

Jill and Vivien found him the ideal chum and
companion on their moorland rambles, and
when they took a picnic lunch and went farther
afield, to St. Ives, perhaps, or Penzance, his
lovely car more than made up for the loss of poor
little Eric, that had had to be sold as old iron.

So the days went on, the only things to mark
their passing being the lengthening grey twilight
and the blossoming of the May.

All this time there was no reply from the
publisher to Miss Merrick's letter of apology
about the broken appointment.  He had not
returned the book, which Mr. Middleton thought
a good sign, but why on earth, if he were going
to buy it, did he find it too much trouble to write
and say so, and end this sickening suspense.

Jill watched hopefully for the postman each day, but nothing came, only a left-handed scrawl from Lesley, who was now back at Beechdene for the summer term, finding things horribly dull with no games, and just wishing Jill were there too.

It was rather queer, too, that Mr. Hughes and Auntie Pam seemed to find so much to write to each other about, and Vivien was evidently in the secret, for she looked so mischievous as she parried her young chum's questions.

One evening, when she was supposed to be hurrying into bed, Jill wandered into Vivien's room with a hairbrush in her hand. She crossed to the window and stood watching the soft afterglow of sunset fading to a dusky dimness on the upland fields. From the garden hedge came faint rustlings and chirpings as sleepy birds settled down, while across the marsh the first bat flitted with silent sweeps.

" I feel in my bones things aren't going on like this for much longer," she said, looking at Vivien, who was already in bed.

The older girl reared herself up. " I know, I've felt it too," she answered. " The sands are running out fast here ! Well," she went on quickly, " I hope we'll always stick together— you and I and Auntie Pam and Lambie—and Squibb ! " she added smiling. " And stay the chums we are."

At that, Jill leaned over the end of the bed, and Vivien wriggled up and stretched out her hand, and they joined little fingers and wished.

But events were nearer even than they thought.

The post next day brought the letter from the Secretary of the Board of Governors at Beechdene Hall, saying that an interview with the headmistress had been arranged for Gillian Ross next Wednesday, if that was quite convenient.

Convenient! Jill counted the days, hours, and minutes that must elapse, and woke up at four in the morning on the great day.

The first thrill was saying good-bye to Lambie and Vivien, and then came the excitement of the long drive down to Beechdene in Mr. Middleton's car. Jill would have enjoyed every minute, had it not been for the impending interview with Miss Harrington.

And then when the girl thought vaguely that there were miles to go still, the car turned in up a long winding drive under an avenue of elms, and drew up before the portico of a low rambling-looking creeper-covered house.

Jill's knees knocked together as she followed her aunt into a lovely panelled hall, for Beechdene had been an old manor house, and had played its part in history. The few minutes of waiting seemed an age, but the interview was not a very formidable one after all.

Miss Harrington, tall, slim, and amazingly young to be a headmistress, said she had heard from Mr. Hughes and Dr. Grant, acting as Jill's sponsors, and that, though the matter must go before the Governors at the next board meeting, she was sure they would raise no difficulty. In her opinion Miss Merrick's niece had more than fulfilled the conditions laid down by the giver of the scholarship, and for her part Miss Harrington would be delighted to welcome Jill at the beginning of the school year in September.

The rest of the interview was rather a blur to Jill after that, but Miss Harrington soon handed them over to a flushed, excited head girl, who quite forgot to be awe-inspiring to this new scholarship candidate, the fame of whose exploits had gone before her.

It was a marvellous school, with wide windows open to the sun, a huge gymnasium, and a separate science block, while the panelled great hall of the old manor had been turned into the dining-room. By the time their tour of inspection ended on the playing-fields, where so many thrilling matches had been won, Jill was counting up the days and weeks that must pass before she could be there enjoying it all.

The next thrill was that Mr. Middleton took Jill, and Lesley, by special permission, out to a most festive lunch in the nearest town ; there was a band and lots of waiters darting about, and Jill had lobster and Lesley sampled three different sorts of ices.  And it was nearly tea-time before they turned their faces towards home, where Vivien and Lambie were eagerly looking out for them.

It really seemed too wonderful to be true, and every day as she watched for the postman Jill turned hot and cold, for surely—surely the Board of Governors would never decide that she was not eligible after all, and dash her hopes to the ground?

# CHAPTER XXIV

### EVERYTHING HAPPENS AT ONCE

ONE May morning a few days later, when the first pinky glow of sunrise lit up the hawthorn hedge below her window, Aunt Pamela woke with a little laugh of pure happiness and jumped out of bed. She ran across to the window, flung up the sash, and poked her head out. On a sloe tree near a blackbird poured forth his morning song, while every minute the shimmer of dawn behind the hills grew brighter.

" I can't stay in with the whole world made new and that darling bird singing his Grace for the beauty of it all ! " she cried as she turned back into the room and dressed quickly.

A minute or two later Miss Merrick crept downstairs and opened the hall door. She crossed the dewy lawn, slipped through the little white gate, and went slowly down to the marsh. Sleepy cows came squelching out of the reeds to stare at her with their great soft eyes, and the brook, running high after all the rain, sang a harsh song of its own.

In the little copse up the valley the primroses

were all gone and the twigs of the alders budded with soft young leaf, while under foot, like a fairy mantle, was a carpet of bluebells. The heady fragrance of them came to her like wine, birds hushed their song, and a long bar of sunlight shot through the interlacing branches overhead to light up the heavenly blue at her feet.

And then, as Pamela Merrick pushed through a gap in the undergrowth, she bit back a little cry, for she was not alone.

Some one had got there before her.

And so Keith Middleton asked his Pamela to marry him in the little copse beside the rushing stream, while all round blossomed wild hyacinths more blue than the southern sea lapping the shore where his villa stood.

Later, how much later it was she never knew, Miss Merrick was standing at the small white gate saying good-bye. Her eyes were full of a solemn joy, and her cheeks were still flushed ; they had known and loved one another so long that the few words he said were only like the keystone of the arch. It was settled long before ; it had been inevitable ever since the day when he had come in his car to find her again in her shabby house.

Pamela Merrick turned and crept into the house very softly, as if it were all too wonderful to be real.

*Some one had got there before her.*

As she crossed the hall she started.

" Oh, how you made me jump ! " she cried,
finding Mrs. Lambert standing in the kitchen
doorway.  She stretched out her hand.  Lambie

propped her broom quickly against the wall and squeezed Miss Merrick's fingers hard. She did not need to wait to be told the good news.

"Oh, if only my own dear lady were here to see this day!" cried Mrs. Lambert; "and I wish you and the gentleman every happiness."

Then they heard a swift scamper of feet overhead, and looked up to see Vivien in her dressing-gown craning over the banisters. "My hat, Lambie! You don't mean it's breakfast time!" she cried.

"Not yet awhile. Though it's eight o'clock and past," replied Lambie, and bustled off as the girl scuttled back to her room.

Jill and Vivien were soon ready, though breakfast was unaccountably late, and the table was not even laid when they came down to the dining-room. Miss Merrick was sitting on the shabby sofa with her nervous hands knotted in her lap. A long shaft of sunlight slanted in and turned her brown hair to gold as she looked up, radiant with happiness, when they entered the room.

"Auntie! you do look awfully, spiffingly glad!" cried Jill as Miss Merrick stretched out her arms.

They ran to her, and she drew them closer as she told them shyly that they must call Mr. Middleton Uncle Keith now, as she was going to be married to him. There was something in her manner now that made them both feel awkward and a little awed.

Jill's brain whirled, thoughts and questions raced through it, yet she could not think of anything to say. Vivien's eyes widened till they seemed to fill her face ; she pressed her hands together till the knuckles showed white, but she did not say anything either.

Aunt Pamela flushed painfully. The words, " Won't you kiss me and say you're a tiny bit pleased ? " were on her lips, but she could not say them. Abruptly she sprang to her feet and almost ran out of the room.

All at once the girls found they could talk again.

" It makes me feel queer," said Vivien as she flopped on to a chair and rumpled up her hair in a bewildered way.

" So it does me ! " mumbled Jill ungrammatically. " There didn't seem much to say—somehow."

" I would have liked," said Vivien softly, " to have given Pam a hug, and told her how glad I am ; but I felt like a fish out of water for a minute, and when I could collect my wits she had gone." Then the girl paused and bit her lip. " Yes, I suppose I'm glad," she said. " It will be—queer, though ! "

" What's the matter ? " Jill looked at her, puzzled. " You sound almost as if you were hating the idea, all of a sudden."

" So I am ! " answered Vivien abruptly. " Don't you see it means I shall have to get another post ! "

Jill looked thunderstruck. " My hat ! " she gasped.

" Oh yes, I'm as glad for Pam as I can be," went on Vivien vehemently ; " but the selfish part of me keeps on saying, ' She won't want a secretary any more ! ' And she won't, that's certain. It's quite different for you. You are Pam's niece, and anyhow, you'll probably be at school all term time. But I'm nobody's niece ; and I've no one—and nowhere."

And then poor Vivien's whole face twisted as she gasped out, " And I love Pam—and it would break my heart to take another job with strange people ! "

" Don't be an ijjut ! " Jill flashed back almost crossly. " There you go, turning on the water works before you're even certain Auntie won't want you ! "

But Vivien refused to be comforted, and with her face buried in a cushion, she cried stormily. At last she raised her head. " Perhaps Pam will write to me sometimes ! " she said.

" Owl ! " exploded Jill. " I could shake you,

but I won't, because I'm going this minute to fetch Auntie Pam to do it for me."

And before Vivien, appalled, could jump up and stop her, Jill was out of the room and across the hall.

Miss Merrick stood just inside the front door with her horn-rimmed spectacles on her nose, reading a closely typewritten, rather legal-looking document that had evidently just come. She looked up, and cried excitedly, as soon as she saw Jill, " Oh, darling, what a thrilling post this is ! There's a letter from Miss Harrington to say that the Beechdene governors have awarded you the Faith Anderson scholarship. The first time it's been won for seven years ! Oh, Jill, I'm proud ! "

Everything else was forgotten as Jill flung her arms round her aunt's neck, " I can't believe it ! " she cried.

" Let go, you're choking me ! " cried Auntie Pam. " Leave me a little breath, and I'll tell you what this other letter is about."

As delighted as a child, Miss Merrick waved the other envelope in front of her niece's astonished eyes.

" It's from the publisher ! " guessed Jill.

" Yes ! He not only wants to publish my book, but also wants to buy the film rights ! We'll all go and see it when it's on in town, won't we ? "

" Everything is happening at once ! " shrilled

Jill, as she began to dance up and down. Then suddenly she remembered what Vivien had said, and some of the happiness left her face. " Yes, Auntie," she said slowly, " lots of lovely things are happening—to you and me—but poor old Vivien thinks she'll have to get another job ! "

Miss Merrick, feeling that she must laugh or she would burst out crying, suddenly bent her head in her two hands, " Oh, the silly child ! " she exclaimed. " What a mare's nest she has made up to frighten herself with."

Jill turned in a flash. " Let me run and tell her, Auntie ! She was crying, you know ! "

But Miss Merrick was quicker than Jill. " Wait here ! I'll explain to her," she said. " Oh, my poor little chum, I never thought you would dream I could change to you ! "

As she turned the handle of the dining-room door she heard the sound of stifled, bitter sobbing. The girl, huddled in a forlorn heap on the big arm-chair, was weeping her heart out. Pamela Merrick could not speak for a minute, even to comfort her. Instead, she crossed the room, dropped on her knees beside Vivien and put her arms round her.

" Oh, you little goose ! What a coil of trouble you've made up out of nothing ! " she exclaimed.

Vivien turned and nuzzled her tear-stained face down on to her friend's shoulder. " Pam,

I know I'm being silly," she gasped out between difficult, sobbing breaths ; " but, please don't send me away ! "

" Let go of my neck, child ! You're strangling me ! I thought perhaps you would like to go——"

" Never ! " interrupted Vivien passionately. " You're like my own Mummie—whom I can just remember. I couldn't take another job now ! " She broke off with a shudder.

A sudden dimness swept over Miss Merrick's eyes. She understood how those first weeks after her father died had left their imprint on the girl's mind for ever.

" You poor wee soul," she murmured, kissing her. " My house is your home, and you'll never leave it while I live. Unless perhaps you would like to go and study art in Paris for a time. . . ." She broke off and smiled invitingly.

" Oh ! Pam ! " Vivien drew away from Miss Merrick's clasp and stared at her with wide, almost frightened eyes. " I can't believe it ! That's too good to be true ! Fancy, to see Paris again ! "

" Yes, we'll go over together, and I'll find you a studio. You see, I've got some money now, and I want to give you the chance with your painting that I never had with my violin," Miss Merrick went on, softly stroking the hand she held.

" Money ! " gasped Vivien, too astonished to be tactful. " How on earth did you get that ? "

" A big cheque for advance royalties on my book came this morning, and they're going to film it as well ! Long may they live—those publishers ! "

Vivien's eyes were starry as she looked up into her friend's face. She could not find words ; she knew Miss Merrick was going to spend money on her, earned with grinding days of work.

" Giving me the chance she has never had herself—the darling ! Oh please, God," Vivien thought, a little prayer in her mind, " help me to do well and please Pam—and always be her friend."

Pamela Merrick's eyes were dancing with excitement. " And what I've told you is not the half of the lovely things we're going to do ! " she cried. " Wait ; and I'll tell you some more surprises when I've called Jill ! "

She went out of the room and called to the other girl.

" Come along, Jill ! Uncle Keith has got a plan for us all. Wouldn't you like to hear it ? "

Laughing mischievously, she prolonged the anticipation till they were all seated together on the big sofa. And then she told them.

" So that's your plan," said Vivien, awestruck, a few minutes later. " We are all going to

Uncle Keith's villa in the south of France! And it's to be our home to come back to on our holidays—Jill from Beechdene and I from Paris. Oh, Pam, when will we start to pack?"

"Very soon," smiled Miss Merrick. "Keith and I are getting married almost at once. We've nothing to wait for," she added happily. As she spoke Aunt Pamela saw for an instant a dress of gleaming white and a soft cloud-like veil. Two bridesmaids, Vivien and Jill, would follow her up the aisle of the grey ancient church on the hill. Afterwards there would be a happy party at the little white house, with a few old friends to see her cut the wedding cake and wish her well. Then there would be handshakes, kisses, and good-byes. Kind old Lambie would keep the girls company after Keith had driven her away for the honeymoon tour he had promised her.

Jill's voice broke in upon her aunt's reverie. "And what will Lambie do if we go to France?" she asked shyly, feeling in her heart of hearts that nothing would be perfect unless her dear Nannie were there to share in the happiness.

"Dear old Lambie! I want her to come and help run the villa," answered Auntie Pam. "Will she come, do you think, and mother us all?"

"Lambie will stay with us for keeps!" replied Jill softly. "She promised me! Go on, please, Auntie!"

" Ours will be the loveliest home," continued Miss Merrick with a dreamy look in her wide eyes. " Keith described the place to me till he made me see the white stuccoed walls, and the green shutters shading the wide cool rooms. It is built high above the sea, on a hillside all cut away into terraces, and the garden drops down to a little cove, where one can swim ! "

Vivien's eyes were aglow. She could picture it all. It was almost unbearable happiness to think she should see again the south she loved. Daddy's south !

" We'll always like this queer white house on the sands, won't we, darlings ? " Miss Merrick went on in a low voice. " But after all we'll only be leaving the shell, for Keith says even Squibb is to come too."

Hearing his name, the fat old spaniel, who was stretched out on his side in a patch of sunlight, wagged his tail and got up. Gently stroking his glossy head, Auntie Pam ended rapturously, " Isn't it the loveliest plan ? "

" We're dreaming ! " Vivien shook her head as if she found it too wonderful to take in all at once, but Jill exclaimed, " I'll be the happiest girl in the whole of Beechdene School ! "

Then there came the rattle of crockery, and Lambie, with the breakfast tray in her hands, pushed the door wide. Jill danced up to her crying, " We're all going to live in Uncle Keith's villa in France. And it won't be home a bit if you don't come."

" Villa in France ! Whatever are you chattering about, duckie ? " exclaimed Mrs. Lambert as she set the laden tray on the table, and then turned and looked inquiringly at Miss Merrick. And before Auntie Pam had time to explain what Jill had meant, or even to ask Lambie properly, the kind old soul said, as Jill had known she would, " Yes, miss, I'll come to the world's end if you want me ! "

" Hip, hip, hurrah ! " cried Jill and Vivien at the tops of their voices as they caught hands and danced round and round, while Squibb sprang up and barked till the room rang.

THE END

PRINTED IN GREAT BRITAIN AT
THE PRESS OF THE PUBLISHERS